Harlequin Romances

OTHER
Harlequin Romances
by HENRIETTA REID

The Tartan Ribbon

by

HENRIETTA REID

Harlequin Books

TORONTO • LONDON • NEW YORK • AMSTERDAM • SYDNEY • WINNIPEG

Original hardcover edition published in 1976
by Mills & Boon Limited

ISBN 0-373-02049-X

Harlequin edition published March 1977

Printed in Canada

CHAPTER ONE

WHEN the bus drew up, Miranda found that she was the only passenger to get off. But then most people visiting Drumdarrow Castle would travel there by car she surmised. Only two buses per day passed through the tiny village, both of them in the afternoon. And her budget had been planned so stringently that there had not been the smallest possibility of taking a taxi from her hotel in Stirling.

With a growing sense of excitement she approached the massive gates beneath a high stone archway on which a crumbling coat-of-arms could still be faintly discerned. A great, wide drive led through arching trees, birds darted through the tangles of foliage and on either side stood banks of rustling bracken and rowan trees laden with bunches of crimson berries. Thorny briars crawled close to the ground and the sound of a burn gurgling over rocky ledges came to her from the woods beyond.

She felt the familiar thrill of anticipation. Soon the castle must come in sight. According to the guide book, this was the last day it would be on public view, before closing for the winter months.

She must make the most of the short time she would be here, for on the following day she would be leaving Scotland, and her short tour of its ancient homes would have come to an end.

But it had been an unforgettable experience!

Thank goodness, she had not listened to her

friends, who had thought her plans highly unusual and even eccentric.

After all, they had argued, there were surely better ways of spending Cousin Agnes's small legacy than in surveying fusty old castles. But none of their alternative suggestions had aroused Miranda to much enthusiasm. After her tour of historic houses, they had prophesied, she would be only too glad to head south and leave Scotland with its misty mountains and soft rains far behind her.

It was true, of course, that it did rain a lot! But it only served to make the little burns babble more happily in their ferny hollows and the mosses to grow thick and velvety-green on the granite boulders. And any doubts Miranda might have harboured before she set off had been rapidly dissipated.

Sketchbook in hand, she had found herself happily engrossed in recording the detail of antique candelabra that particularly appealed to her, the line of an ancient, twisting staircase, or an arched courtyard.

Already she had seen such places as Culzean Castle; the royal palace of Linlithgow in which Mary Queen of Scots had been born; and Glamis Castle with its dark towers, sinister and brooding as an illustration to a Grimm's fairy-tale. She had also seen Scone Palace where, in ancient times, the Scottish kings had been crowned: its French furniture and collection of exquisite ivories had fascinated her.

Yes, she had certainly made an excellent decision when she had elected to spend Cousin Agnes's little legacy on a trip around Scotland's ancient and beautiful homes.

She had looked forward to visiting Drumdarrow Castle from the start of her odyssey, for she had read

6

so often of the treasures it contained: rare paintings, pieces of sculpture and, most interesting to Miranda, a collection of exquisite and historic jewels.

This little break after completing her studies at art school and before taking up a job as designer of jewellery was a combination of business and pleasure. Her only regret was that on the following day she must start south and leave misty and romantic Scotland behind.

But now the arching trees had given way to a vast expanse of rounded cobbles. Drumdarrow Castle stood before her, turreted and crenellated, outlined against the sky across which storm clouds had begun to race, like an advancing army.

This backdrop seemed to add to the majesty of the old castle, but Miranda felt her heart sink. The morning had promised a beautiful, dry day with no more than an early autumn tang in the air, so she had worn her new acquisition, a kilt-skirt in the brilliant vermilion of the royal Stuart. An extravagance she had found it impossible to resist was her velvet, finger-length coat with silver buttons. It completed the outfit, and when she wore it she felt that it was appropriate as well as comfortable, affording her maximum freedom on her wanderings.

But Scottish weather, as she now knew, could be extremely unpredictable. When she had viewed the castle, would she have to return to the village to catch her bus in one of those sudden, soaking bursts of rain that she had experienced so often? It would be uncomfortable to make the journey back to the hotel drenched to the skin. Apart from that, it would completely ruin her velvet jacket!

With a rush she darted across the wide space,

ducked between the cars that clustered around the door and paused breathless in the great entrance hall with its grey stone walls and massive suits of armour.

Miranda, still a little breathless, found herself tagging along on what she could see was to be the last tour of the house for the day.

She listened attentively but a little impatiently as they progressed from room to room. She knew from the guide-book that the jewels were kept under glass in the famous long gallery and she wanted to see the collection before it became so dark that artificial lighting would be necessary.

To her mounting impatience the guide, evidently feeling that the long gallery was the pièce de résistance of the tour, left it until last, and when they did arrive there directed their attention to the pictures that hung in ornate gilt frames on the dark panelled walls.

But Miranda left the group and drawn as though by a magnet to the display of gems went to gaze down into one of the many glass-topped tables that were ranged along the centre of the shining oak floor.

Eagerly she studied the display, oblivious of the remarks of the guide, who had stopped the party before a portrait of a bewigged dandy.

She drew in her breath with a gasp of delight as her eyes lit upon a sumptuous necklace of sapphires with a great fire opal completing the design. On the card nearby she read that this was part of the collection of jewels that Madame du Barry had brought to England when she had fled from France during the days of the French Revolution. Restlessly her eyes darted about the case. There was a frail and elegant tiara which had been worn by the Empress Josephine; a peacock brooch with ruby eyes, flashing green and blue from emeralds and sapphires; diamond buttons from the coat of an eighteenth-century dandy.

She was re-reading the accompanying cards and was about to make a lightning sketch of the setting of the tiara when her ear was caught by a remark of the guide. To her surprise, she found that the party had moved on and was now quite some distance from her, but clearly she caught the words, '... and he is said to haunt this gallery at dusk, so perhaps we had better move on rather rapidly.'

There was a little burst of appreciative laughter from the guests at this well-rehearsed patter and Miranda, intrigued, moved forward to rejoin the group.

She found herself looking up into a portrait of a man in a brocaded coat, his waistcoat embroidered in silver, at his feet a little dog looking up at him. Under the tricorn hat his powdered hair was tied back with a black ribbon and he gazed down at them, his eyes full of mocking laughter. It was a devil-may-care face, full of fun and adventure, and the thought flashed through Miranda's mind that it must have been intriguing to know someone like that. It was hard to believe he had been dead for at least two hundred years, the bright sardonic glance was so full of life and daring.

'The story is a romantic one,' the guide was saying, 'and his end came here in this very gallery, so it is hardly surprising that it has the reputation of being haunted.'

At this a little shiver seemed to pass through the group around him and Miranda could not but feel that he was highly pleased at the effect his words were having. Obviously this was a story which would always have its best effect when told in the slight dusk

9

of a September evening, she was thinking.

'Yes, he and another gentleman of the neighbourhood fell in love with the same girl, a famous beauty, but a notorious flirt. Colin invited his rival to dinner. They had their meal here alone before the fire. Afterwards, he challenged him to a duel to the death. At first all went well for Colin, but in the end he was defeated; he killed his opponent, but was fatally wounded and died here in the long gallery. The story goes that it was only after his death that the lady realised that Colin was the man she truly loved and that she died shortly afterwards of a broken heart.'

'Well, all I can say is that I'm glad to think this tour will be over before it grows dark,' one lady said, in mock terror, and the others laughed.

They moved on down the gallery and Miranda returned to her inspection of the cases. Absorbed, sketching whatever interested her, she wended her way from table to table, studying the contents.

One of the items was an exquisite oval miniature of Clementine Sobieski, the Polish princess who became Bonnie Prince Charlie's mother. It was edged by matched pearls, two of which, Miranda noticed, were missing. There was also a silver filigree hair ornament to which in Regency days egret feathers had been attached. It was as she was sketching the design of this that she noticed that the gallery was quite silent. The voice of the guide had long since faded away, and now it was growing quite dusk. She glanced at her watch and gave a gasp of horror. The bus would be passing through the village in about ten minutes, and she had first of all to find her way out of the castle and to make her way along the long drive to the road.

She seized up her sketch-book and pencil and began

to run along the gleaming floor of the gallery, her foot-steps echoing in the high arched roof. Her pencil slipped from her grasp, and before she could draw to a halt it had rolled beneath her feet and she had fallen violently to the floor, her leg twisted under her, a burning pain in her ankle.

Painfully she dragged herself over to a stone window-seat and sank upon it.

Outside, rain lashed against the leaded windows and as she glanced along the length of the gallery she was amazed to see how dark it had grown; the alcoves folded in dense shadows.

Engrossed in the contents of the cases, she had allowed herself to become separated from the rest of the party.

What was she to do? Any minute now her bus would pass through the village. If she missed it she simply could not afford a taxi back to her hotel.

She called out, at first rather quietly and then more loudly, feeling a growing despair as she realised that in this unfrequented part of the house she couldn't possibly be heard.

From her perch she had a view over trees of the road which ran outside the walls and in a little while her heart sank as she saw the bus, its windows lit against the dusk of the evening, pass along the road and disappear around a bend. There was nothing she could do but wait to be found—probably not until morning!

It was then she heard a soft insistent tapping which seemed to come from the window behind her. She strained her eyes, but could see nothing there in the shadows. She must keep a tight grip on her nerves, if she were to be alone here all night, she told herself.

11

Gingerly she put her foot down on the floor, but a sharp pain knifed through her leg and she quickly returned to her perch on the window-seat.

Sitting curled up and taut with apprehension, it was easy to imagine that from the shadows there came the soft rustle of silks and rich brocades. The story that the guide had told with an air of dry scepticism was not now too difficult to believe. Somewhere in the gloom of panelled walls and tapestried alcoves perhaps the first Laird was surveying her, his lean sardonic face mocking her fears.

Once again she heard the soft, insistent tapping. It seemed to come from outside the mullioned window and with a shiver of horror she remembered the story of the Meggernie ghost.

She had heard it when she had visited Meggernie Castle, a beautiful fifteenth-century building half way up Glen Lyon in Perthshire. It was said that it was haunted by a beautiful apparition whose pale tragic face could be seen watching guests through a window. Should she turn her head to find the cause of the tapping would her eyes be met by a white, spectral face pressed against the window?

She forced herself to look towards the window and saw with a gasp of relief that the sound was being caused by a bare, skeletal branch blown by wind and torrential rain against the latticed window. How stupid she had been to allow herself to become terrified by her imagination! All the same, she must leave this cold seat and try to find her way out.

But when she again tentatively placed her foot on the floor she was reminded that for some time to come she must remain on her cold stone perch.

It was then that she heard the sound of creaking

wood, and before her terrified gaze the panel across the gallery seemed to open and a tall figure appeared outlined in a halo of light.

The shadowed profile seemed familiar and she thought she detected a mocking gleam in the eyes. For a moment she thought she was being confronted with the spectre of the first Laird and her nerves, already worn thin, failed her completely. She gave a piercing scream that echoed and reverberated along the gallery.

Before she could draw breath for a second scream the figure had darted towards her and a hard and all-too-human hand was placed over her mouth.

'Be quiet, you little fool!' a voice commanded harshly. 'What on earth is the matter with you?'

Miranda gazed up, her eyes wide and terrified, the lower part of her face still under the firm grasp of the stranger.

The figure before her was reassuringly dressed in sports shirt and jacket, although the face that gazed fiercely into hers had something of the sharp, imperious features of the man in the portrait.

She felt relief flood her and, as though he sensed that she was no longer in danger of giving vent to further screams, the hand was removed from her mouth.

'Sorry!' she said sheepishly. 'But I thought at first you were the man in the portrait.'

'The man in the portrait?' He gazed at her blankly. 'What on earth are you raving about, my girl?'

'I mean,' Miranda told him with dignity, 'I thought you were the ghost of the first Laird. The guide had been telling us how he fought a duel, and——'

She was interrupted by a burst of loud and what she considered extremely ill-mannered laughter.

13

'Did you really take all that bunk seriously?'

'You mean that the first Laird didn't fight a duel in the gallery? That the story was deliberately made up?' she asked indignantly.

'No, it's true enough! But as far as I'm aware, after his demise he didn't prowl the long gallery. In fact, we're disappointingly non-haunted here at Drumdarrow. But aren't we rather getting away from the point?'

She noted uneasily the unmistakable hint of steel in his tone. 'What do you mean?' she asked unconvincingly.

'I think it's time we got a little light on the subject of what you're doing here.' Crossing to an alcove, he pulled a switch and immediately the gallery was flooded with light scintillating from crystal chandeliers.

Miranda blinked in the sudden illumination, then watched with growing apprehension as he caught sight of her sketch-book where it had slipped beneath an ornate ebony cabinet.

In silence he picked it up and turned the pages, slowly studying each sketch intently.

'So that's it!' he said harshly. 'You've carefully recorded the best and most valuable pieces. May I congratulate you on your unerring taste?'

Then, tossing the sketch-book contemptuously beside her, he made a swift inspection of the display tables.

'The pieces you have sketched are still intact,' he remarked when he rejoined her. 'No doubt your talents have been employed for the future guidance of your accomplices.'

'But that's not so——' Miranda began.

'You may as well tell me the truth,' he interrupted.

14

'Just who are you? And what are you doing here at this time?'

As he spoke he grasped her by the wrist and pulled her violently towards him, and Miranda gasped as once again pain lanced up from her now swollen foot.

He glanced at her sharply and Miranda had the satisfaction of knowing that he was disconcerted by her reaction. As he eased her back on to the window-seat, he said gruffly, 'Don't bother trying on your little games with me, for you'll be wasting your time. It so happens that I'm responsible for all this stuff while the owner is abroad and I've no intention of letting myself be hoodwinked by a pretty face or a pathetic story. Just who are you, and what are you doing here?'

'That's exactly what I've been trying to tell you, but you chose to jump to conclusions,' she informed him severely. 'If you want to know who I am——'

'I most certainly do.'

'My name is Miranda Lorimer,' she announced with dignity. 'And I'm a designer of jewellery—or I shall be when I get a job,' she added hastily. 'I heard there was a wonderful collection of gems and historic jewellery at Drumdarrow, so I included it among the historic houses I intended to visit with Cousin Agnes's legacy.'

He sat down beside her and regarded her steadily— just as if, she decided, she was a rare and strange bird which had flown through one of the windows of the long gallery and perched on the window-seat.

He had, she noted, brown eyes faintly speckled with green. Now that she saw him at close quarters she decided that his resemblance to the first Laird of Drumdarrow was very superficial. It was true, he had somewhat the same sharp, arrogant features and the eyes too could look as mocking and sardonic as those in the portrait. But there was an important difference! It was impossible to imagine the eyes in the portrait ever looking gentle and grave and faintly whimsical.

He studied her with unconcealed curiosity. 'We'll leave Cousin Agnes out of it for the moment! The fact that you intend to take a job as a designer of jewellery doesn't explain what you're doing here, when the castle is officially closed.'

'I forgot all about closing hours,' she admitted. 'The jewels are so fabulous and have such romantic histories that I'm afraid I became completely engrossed and didn't notice how late it was. Then, when I realised I was going to miss the bus as it passed through the village, I ran along the gallery, and——'

'And came a cropper! Mrs Gilmore takes a great pride in her floors and I'm afraid the compliments she receives on their high gloss go to her head and drive her to ever greater heights. I hope you don't intend to sue my cousin,' he added gravely.

But Miranda, deciding that he was quietly mocking her, elected to ignore the remark.

'Your cousin owns Drumdarrow?' she asked.

He nodded. 'Yes—except that he's really only a second cousin. He's elderly and rather an invalid, and intends to spend the rest of his life in Italy. Anyway, he professes to hate the place. According to him it's cold, and depressing, and Scottish weather is abominable. Anyway, he prefers a life in the sun.'

'You don't feel that way about it?' she inquired.

'I'm Graham Lairdlaw, the poor relation! I manage the place for him while he's away and keep things ship-shape—which, by the way, is just as well for you!

If I were not such a conscientious character and had not decided to take a last look round, you'd probably have spent the night here, frightening yourself to death. And now,' he added briskly, 'I think it's time I took you to more comfortable quarters and had a look at your foot.'

It was so plain that he expected no opposition to his plan that immediately Miranda's independent spirit rebelled.

'I'm quite all right,' she told him primly. 'But as I've missed the last bus to Stirling, I'd be glad if you'd phone for a taxi.'

He flung back his head and gave a peal of laughter that resounded along the gallery.

Miranda sat bolt upright, her eyes sparkling angrily. 'I don't see anything funny about asking for a taxi!'

'Nor would there be anything funny about it, my girl—except that there isn't one.'

'I saw a garage as we drove into the village,' she protested.

'Of course you did. But it so happens that they haven't a licence to run a taxi. No, I'm afraid if you want to leave the grim and haunted fortress of Drumdarrow, you'll have to beg a lift.'

She regarded him intently, wondering how best she could approach him about driving her to her hotel. It would be impossible to suggest payment, yet it would equally be impossible to make a blunt request. She frowned thoughtfully as she pondered how most diplomatically to approach the matter.

'And does that intriguing little pucker between your eyes mean that you're scheming how to persuade me to convey you to your hotel tonight? If so, you can desist immediately,' Graham Lairdlaw told her coolly.

17

'Oh!' Miranda exclaimed.

She was startled by his blunt refusal, and hoped her 'oh' sounded cool and detached, instead of flustered and embarrassed.

'I haven't the slightest intention of driving you miles through a torrential downpour just because you've been behaving like a silly and romantic schoolgirl, getting all starry-eyed over some wretched queen's jewels. Let this be a lesson to you! The next house you visit, you'll take good care not to dawdle.'

'There won't be a next house,' Miranda told him, realising as she did so how depressed she felt at the idea. 'I'm going home tomorrow.'

'All the more reason for not spending your last night in Scotland driving through a downpour,' he said briskly; as without the slightest warning he picked her up in his arms and carried her across the gallery towards the door in the panelling through which he had first appeared.

Once inside, Miranda realised that the glow which had surrounded his head and which had added to his spectral appearance had been caused by the modern lighting. For, although panelled, the room was covered with wall-to-wall carpeting and was illuminated by écru-shaded wall-lamps.

Dismayed as she was at being borne off in this cavalier manner, Miranda could not but feel relief as the warm air of the centrally heated rooms began to soak into her chilled bones. This was a welcome change from the darkness and penetrating cold of the long gallery.

The door, when closed, would be almost impossible to detect, she was thinking, its panelled surface matching the walls.

'Quite a handy idea, that door in the gallery, when the laird had to do a quick disappearing act,' Graham Lairdlaw said, grinning down at her.

Miranda stared up at him in glacial silence.

Soon she found herself in a comfortably small room. It too was panelled, but in warm, gleaming, honey-tinted tones that made a perfect background for the chesterfield suite covered in glazed chintz. Heavy maroon curtains were drawn over the windows, shutting out the sight of the driving rain, and before the blazing beech-log fire was a thick deerskin rug.

Graham Lairdlaw laid her on the couch and immediately examined her ankle.

'Well, it's certainly very much swollen,' he told her. 'But it's not really a bad sprain, I'd say. Perhaps an ice-pack would give you relief. I'll have the housekeeper give us some ice.'

He crossed to the chimneypiece and pulled down on a white porcelain wall-bell and in a little while a short, plump woman with a round, rosy face which still bore traces of prettiness came in. Her eyes widened with astonishment as she caught sight of Miranda leaning back on the sofa, her legs stretched along its length.

At the woman's startled gaze, Graham Lairdlaw said lightly, 'Mrs Gilmore, I want you to meet a young burglar I discovered lurking in the shadows of the long gallery. It was quite obvious she was up to dirty work, so I arrested her on the spot.' As Mrs Gilmore's eyes widened even further, he went on, 'Well, not exactly a burglar—let's say an over-enthusiastic visitor! She became so engrossed in our collection of jewels that she was lost and found herself left behind when the others had gone. I think that's very flattering, don't you?'

'Well, I'm sure I don't know about that!' Mrs Gilmore sniffed doubtfully. 'Visitors are very nice, of course, but——'

'But Drumdarrow was better when we had the place to ourselves,' Graham Lairdlaw finished for her, with a grin.

'Well, you know, Mr Graham, I'm not all that happy about people traipsing about the place,' Mrs Gilmore told him.

'Well, never mind! It's all over till next spring! At least there's one thing the visitors have managed to achieve! Nowadays we keep the floors in prime form. Too much so! Because Miss Lorimer slipped and sprained her ankle.'

Instantly Mrs Gilmore was all solicitude. 'Dear me,' she exclaimed, her eyes on Miranda's swollen ankle, 'that must be very painful. And to think it happened on the gallery floor!'

'What would you say to a cold compress, Mrs Gilmore? Some crushed ice might bring down the swelling, don't you think?'

Mrs Gilmore nodded sagely. 'Yes, I think it would be a good idea. I'll get it right away, and some bandages too, while I'm at it.'

She bustled out of the room.

'Well, now that that's arranged, what about your telling me all about yourself? You did, if I recall rightly, mention that you had an Aunt Agatha.'

'Cousin Agnes,' Miranda corrected frostily. 'And I don't see what concern it is of yours.'

He raised his eyebrows. 'Oh, but it is! Here am I with a strange and remarkably pretty girl in my own private sanctum, and I don't know a thing about her.'

'I'd like to point out that I didn't ask you to whisk me up and bring me here,' Miranda reminded him.

'You mean you'd have preferred to spend the night on a cold, stone slab?' he asked with an air of interest.

'I mean,' Miranda returned furiously, 'that if, as you say, it's impossible to get a taxi, you might have the decency to——' She stopped, realising that, in her anger, she had let her tongue run away with her, and that she had been on the point of stating bluntly that she had expected him to drive her to her hotel.

'I know exactly what you had in mind,' he said, and for the first time she thought she detected a hint of irritation in his voice. 'You thought I'd act the gentleman and politely offer to drive you to your hotel. Well, you may as well realise I'm no knight in shining armour. Did you think I was going to set out on a long, dreary drive through torrential rain, just because a pretty girl was silly enough to dawdle about when everyone else cleared out? And now will you tell me just who Cousin Agnes is and what she has to do with your visiting Drumdarrow?'

For a moment Miranda considered preserving a dignified silence. After all, her affairs were none of this man's business.

But the green-speckled eyes regarding her were no longer amused; in fact, they had a steely quality that warned her that he was in no mood for prevarication.

'After my parents died, Cousin Agnes brought me up,' she began reluctantly. 'It was she who put me through art school. She wasn't very well off, but when she died she left me a small legacy. There were no strings attached: she stipulated that I was to do exactly what I wished with the money. But then she was that kind of person.'

21

Miranda paused. In spite of all her efforts, her lips quivered and her eyes misted. She blinked the tears away. Cousin Agnes, in her undemonstrative way, would have been extremely acerbic at any display of emotion in front of a stranger.

'You may have a good cry, if you like,' her companion said quietly, and she found a large white handkerchief being placed between her fingers.

She pushed it away. 'Thanks! I've no intention of having a good cry,' she replied sharply.

He took his handkerchief and tucked it carefully into his pocket, shaking his head reprovingly.

'It's as I suspected! You're determined to be one of those independent girls who travel around the world with a knapsack and practise karate on any unsuspecting males they encounter.'

Miranda tried to suppress a giggle at this highly-coloured version of her excursions.

'I decided to use my windfall on a tour of Scotland's historic homes. There's nothing very exciting about that.'

'Oh, but isn't there!' he said solemnly. 'In that case, why aren't you in your hotel, tucked up in bed, instead of in a strange man's sitting-room, casually reclining on his sofa?'

CHAPTER TWO

'Oh!' Miranda sat bolt upright and felt the colour flood her cheeks. Somehow she hadn't thought of it in that way, but she had to admit that he had been merely stating the facts. She *was* in a strange man's home, and she *was* reclining on his sofa.

In an effort to regain her composure, she said, crossly, 'If the display had been properly kept up, I probably shouldn't have done so much dawdling, as you call it.'

He wrinkled his brows. 'I'm afraid I just don't see the connection.'

'Some of the exhibits have been very badly neglected,' she informed him severely. 'Many of them need cleaning, to begin with, and some are damaged, or have stones missing. For instance, two pearls are missing from the miniature of the Princess Sobieski. I was making a mental note of all the work that would have to be done, if I were in charge of the display. That's really what delayed me.'

'I see.' He sounded thoughtful. 'So you're not exactly overcome with enthusiasm for the Drumdarrow collection, is that it?'

'Oh no, it's not that!' she assured him quickly. 'It's simply wonderful! And I wouldn't have missed it for worlds! But I expect, as you're not the real owner, you just don't take much interest in the collection.'

She saw his face darken and realised that her remark had been gauche and awkward.

'The fact that I don't own the collection has nothing whatsoever to do with it: I'm still a Lairdlaw.

23

I don't possess one acre of Drumdarrow, but I take the same care of it as if it were my own. If the collection has been neglected, it's simply because there's no one here capable of taking charge of it, and keeping it up to scratch. You must realise,' he added dryly, 'that in these parts there are very few people with your particular qualifications.'

For a moment he regarded her thoughtfully. 'You wouldn't consider taking the job on, would you?'

She regarded him in blank amazement. 'But that's ridiculous,' she said at last.

'Why? Why do you consider it ridiculous?' he asked impatiently, as though irritated by her obtuseness. 'After all, it's not as if you had a job lined up! There's nothing to take you back to England immediately.' Then, after a slight pause, he added, 'Or is there?'

'I'm not sure I know what you're talking about,' Miranda answered warily.

'Well, for instance, you're not engaged, or anything, are you?'

'No, I'm not engaged, or anything—as you elegantly put it,' she said crossly.

It would have been rather nice, at that moment, to have been in the position to flash a large solitaire diamond ring under his arrogant nose.

'I've never pretended to be particularly elegant,' he grinned. 'In olden days the Lairdlaws were rievers, which, in case you don't know, is a polite way of saying they were raiders and outlaws.'

'Considering the way you've behaved, it doesn't surprise me in the least.'

'In that case you shouldn't be upset if, in future, my manners are a little uncouth! And now that that little

24

matter is cleared out of the way, what about it?'

'About what?'

'Now don't pretend you don't know. I'm offering the job of taking care of the collection. You'd be in complete charge.'

For a moment Miranda hesitated. The idea was extremely tempting. It was the type of job she would thoroughly enjoy. But caution made her say, 'You know nothing about me at all. Why on earth should you entrust such a valuable collection to me?'

'Perhaps it's because your nose turns up at the tip and, at times, you look rather like a pixie, one of those solemn, conscientious ones who spend all their time industriously sewing gowns out of cobwebs and star-dust for the Fairy Queen.'

Miranda tried to look severe, but failed dismally. She shook her head reluctantly. 'No, I'm afraid I couldn't take the job on. It's completely out of the question.'

'But why? It's fairly obvious to me that you'd like the work, so why do you insist on turning it down?'

'Well, for one thing, you're not married, are you?' she asked awkwardly.

'No. And I can't imagine what that has to do with the matter.' Then, after a moment's thought, he said in wonderment, 'Surely you're not old-fashioned enough to care whether the neighbours gossip about us or not? Miranda!' he said musingly. 'An old-fashioned name for an old-fashioned girl! You are prim and proper, aren't you, Miss Lorimer?'

Miranda felt a little nettled at this description of herself. 'I'm not at all interested in your opinion of me,' she told him icily.

It was at that point that Mrs Gilmore came in

carrying a basin in which ice cubes rattled; under her arm a roll of bandages.

'Now, Mr Graham, you're not to bully the young lady,' she said reprovingly.

'Me, bully the young lady!' Graham Lairdlaw declaimed, rolling his eyes in repudiation. 'Whatever gave you that idea?'

'Because,' Mrs Gilmore sniffed, 'I've known you since you were a boy, and I can see, by the look on your face, that you're trying to get your own way. Well, don't you pay any attention to him, Miss Lorimer,' she went on, turning to Miranda. 'He thinks he can get his own way every time, no matter how unreasonable he may be.'

'But it's Miranda who's being unreasonable, Mrs Gilmore! She simply won't see how suitable and sensible my suggestion is.'

'And what was the suggestion, if I may ask?' Mrs Gilmore inquired sceptically, as she helped Miranda to roll down her stocking.

As she inserted her foot into the icy water, Miranda shivered, but her attention was diverted as Graham replied: 'Really, you'd think I was asking her to commit some heinous crime! All I suggested was that she stay on as a sort of curator and general factotum, and she turned down the proposition flat.'

'And very sensible of her too, I'd say,' Mrs Gilmore pronounced severely. 'Why, it's out of the question. A pretty young girl staying here, and you a bachelor! What would people say?'

'Really, Mrs Gilmore, we're not back in Victorian times, you know. Girls don't need a chaperon nowadays.'

'It seems to me, it doesn't matter what century

26

you're living in, people talk. And in this village everyone talks about everyone else. Why, in no time, the young lady would have a bad name! I can tell you that! Considering who you are too!'

'Now what do you mean by that?' he demanded.

'You know perfectly well what I mean,' the housekeeper returned. 'There's a lot of the first Laird in you, Mr Graham. It comes down and breaks out now and then in the Lairdlaws in every generation. And who would know better than myself who have known you all your life! Oh yes, besides looking like the Laird, you've got lots of his ways!'

'One would think,' Graham grumbled, 'that you were trying to frighten Miss Lorimer off.'

'That's exactly what I'm doing,' Mrs Gilmore told him. 'But then she's a sensible young girl, and doesn't need me to tell her.'

Graham regarded Miranda thoughtfully. 'What would you say if I were to tell you that an aunt of mine and a cousin were due to arrive tomorrow?'

Miranda cast an inquiring glance at Mrs Gilmore and was surprised to discover the effect this information had had upon her.

Her hands paused in the act of unrolling a strip of muslin. 'What? Mrs Gregg and Miss Shona, tomorrow? And you didn't tell me till now!'

'Considering how you feel about Aunt Esther I didn't exactly look forward to breaking the glad tidings,' he admitted.

'But if I'd known, I'd have got to work right away! You know how particular she is!' Mrs Gilmore fretted.

Miranda could see that the good-natured housekeeper was ordinarily a self-confident, easy-going sort of person, accustomed to running Drumdarrow pretty much as she liked. It was evident that the imminent arrival of Graham's aunt had come as an unpleasant shock.

'You really take Aunt Esther too seriously,' he told her. 'Her bark is worse than her bite. You must know that by this time.'

'I know nothing of the sort,' the housekeeper told him flatly. 'Her bite is every bit as bad as her bark.'

'But to get back to this business of my aunt and cousin being here,' Graham turned once more to Miranda. 'Don't you agree that once they are here the proprieties will be fully observed?'

Miranda looked doubtful. 'I don't know about that,' she began. 'I suppose it depends upon how long they're going to stay. Perhaps this is only to be a flying visit?'

'Nothing of the sort! Aunt Esther has let her house for the next few months and is going to stay here until her tenants have departed.'

'In that case I suppose it will be quite all right for the young lady to stay—that is if she really wishes to,' Mrs Gilmore pronounced. 'And now I think it's time she had a hot cup of tea.'

'Good idea,' Graham agreed. 'And let us have some of your delicious oatcakes while you're at it.'

'I'll fetch it as soon as I've finished bandaging her foot,' the housekeeper promised.

'I'll do that, if you'll see about the tea,' he suggested.

'Very well.' Basin in hand, a worried frown between her brows, Mrs Gilmore hurried from the room.

With a rapid, gentle touch Graham set about completing the bandaging, saying as he did so, 'Poor Mrs

Gilmore, she really detests Aunt Esther's visits. You see, when we're here alone, she runs the house exactly as she wants to. I don't interfere with her arrangements. But Aunt Esther has her own ideas of how a house should be run, with the result that the two women don't get on at all well.'

'Your aunt sounds a pretty——' Miranda hesitated, 'a pretty formidable sort of person.'

Graham laughed as he propped a footstool under her foot. 'Formidable is a light word for Aunt Esther. She's the terror of all who come in her path. Although I must say she and I get on fairly well. I flatter myself she has a soft spot for me—and anyway, I don't put up with any nonsense from her. She respects those who are worthy of her steel.'

At this point Mrs Gilmore came in with tea. Miranda poured and was soon enjoying crisp oatcakes and rich shortbread. It was clear that Mrs Gilmore was an excellent cook.

Afterwards, seated before the cosy fire and feeling slightly drowsy, she was thinking how wonderful it would be not to have to face out again into the elements. Besides, she knew that the job Graham Lairdlaw had offered was ideal for her. If only his story about the arrival of an aunt and cousin was the truth.

'Well, what about it?' he asked, breaking into her thoughts. 'Now that you know you're to have such a formidable chaperon will you not agree to stay?'

'I'd like the job,' she admitted.

'Then you'll say yes?'

The thought that made her decide to accept was the housekeeper's obvious dismay at the news of the impending visit. It was clear that, to her at least, this was no figment of Graham Lairdlaw's imagination.

'Yes, I'd like to take the job,' she decided.

'Good, then I'll have Mrs Gilmore prepare a room for you and get you anything you need for the night.'

When the housekeeper eventually came in for the tray, she told Miranda, 'I've put a fire in your room, because the nights can be chilly at this time of the year. And now, Mr Graham, if you'll lend a hand, I think it's time this young lady went off to bed.'

He picked Miranda up and carried her up a flight of broad oak stairs to a spacious room in which a big fire of beech logs threw warm flickering shadows on the delicate plaster-work of the ceiling.

Before he left he threw on an extra couple of logs, so that bright sparks flew up the wide chimney.

Miranda, supplied by Mrs Gilmore with a voluminous nightgown, was soon asleep in the warmth of the big feather bed.

She awoke suddenly in darkness, aware that a sound like a loud thud had disturbed her, and for a few moments could not remember where she was. Then, before her terrified gaze, a tongue of flame shot into the air and she realised that the noise had been caused by a great log falling out of the fire. The hearthrug was ablaze.

She sprang out of bed and, as her injured foot pressed upon the carpet, gave a cry of pain. It seemed that she was helpless to save herself and stood clutching the foot of her bed, calling for help. Then, as it struck her that the other occupants of Drumdarrow, asleep in distant parts of the great house, were probably unable to hear her, she found herself screaming with terror.

The door was flung open, the lights switched on,

30

and Graham Lairdlaw stood in the doorway surveying the room. He walked across to the chimneypiece, and with the long brass tongs picked up the log of wood and threw it on the fire; then rolling the hearthrug into a tight ball, he smothered the flames.

Crossing the room, he helped Miranda into bed, then sat on the side of it surveying her thoughtfully.

'Really, for a small girl, you have the most amazingly loud screams, the shrillest and most blood-curdling screams I've ever heard!'

'If I hadn't screamed the whole room would have gone up in flames,' she defended herself.

'Well, all I can say is that I'm having very serious second thoughts about asking you to stay on. If this is to continue——'

'It won't continue,' she interrupted. 'Because if your aunt and cousin don't arrive tomorrow I intend to leave.'

'If they don't arrive tomorrow,' he repeated. 'And how am I to guarantee that?'

'What?' Miranda sat up with a start. 'You mean that after all, you don't think they're coming?'

'I didn't say that! What I was about to say—if you'd only give me time—is that with Esther Gregg there's no telling.'

'Well, if she doesn't arrive, I shall——'

'I know. I know.' He held up his hand. 'But you have to make allowances for temperament.'

'Temperament?' Miranda repeated, puzzled.

'Yes. She's a lady of great originality, is Aunt Esther: she likes to do things in her own way and doesn't care to be tied down to dates and times. Should she tell you, for instance, that she will arrive without fail on the twenty-third of the month, you may

31

see her a couple of days earlier, a week later, or not for several months.'

Here he stopped to regard Miranda consideringly. 'Which brings me to the question of how you're going to get along when you do eventually meet. You yourself are what we might call a forthright character. I look forward with interest to seeing the sparks fly.'

'And your cousin?' Miranda inquired. 'What is she like?'

'To begin with, Shona isn't my cousin—or, I should say, not a near one. Although they speak of each other as aunt and niece Esther and Shona are only very distantly related. Esther, you see, had no children of her own and when my uncle died—he had been rather hen-pecked, poor fellow—Esther was rather at a loss for someone to expend her energies on. Shona is the daughter of a distant cousin of Esther's and when her parents died Esther took her into her home. Everyone rather pitied the poor little mite, thinking she'd have an awful life, but curiously it worked out quite well. Esther doted on the child and spoiled her outrageously.'

'Do you mean to say,' Miranda demanded, having had time to think things over, 'that you openly admit that they may not be arriving tomorrow—may not in fact be arriving for days, or even weeks?'

'Dear me, you have a nasty suspicious turn of mind, haven't you? Are you always like this, or is it only that you have doubts of me?' As Miranda made no reply, he went on, 'You know, your character is very different from your appearance. You don't *look* as if you were a horrid, distrustful sort of person.'

'I'm not ordinarily a suspicious sort of person,' Miranda told him.

'Aha, then it's only with me you're on guard.'

'You seem to me to be the sort of person of whom one should be wary,' Miranda told him.

'Now that is because Mrs Gilmore has given me a bad reputation. But that's all in the past, I assure you. I admit that when I was a boy I was a trifle wild, but——'

'I'm not at all surprised to hear it,' she snapped.

'But a few innocent boyish escapades! Surely these should not be held against a man for the rest of his life—especially when he's a reformed character,' he said solemnly.

'Mrs Gilmore doesn't seem to think so.'

'You must pay no attention to what she says. Mrs Gilmore is prejudiced.'

As Miranda shook her head doubtfully at this pronouncement, he stood up with a laugh, saying, 'I wonder if it's safe to leave you now.'

'What do you mean?' she demanded.

'I mean, is it worth my while going to bed when perhaps in a few minutes I shall have to rush out again at the sound of your scream as you imagine you see the grey lady floating about your room, or a headless horseman galloping past your bed.'

'That's not fair,' Miranda began, her cheeks burning with indignation. 'Could I help it if a log fell out of the fire?'

'No, on second thoughts, I suppose it wasn't your fault,' he agreed in a softer tone. 'In fact, the fault was mine for piling the fire too high. However, all's well that ends well! Sleep tight, Miranda!'

The door closed softly behind him and Miranda snuggled down in the soft feather bed.

But now sleep would not come. The rain beat in

gusts against the windows. At other times she heard the strange raucous cries of a bird and a curious barking sound which she took to be that of a fox. In the misty glens and by the sharp rushing burns the strange wild life of Scotland breathed and moved in the darkness. When the day had begun she had not dreamed that it would end in such a surprising manner, and that she would find herself resting in this great room in the castle of Drumdarrow.

Then her mind turned to small niggling concern about her luggage. She had nothing to change into, she was thinking, and would have to appear at breakfast in the kilt-skirt and jacket in which she had arrived. Her once spotlessly white blouse was now slightly grubby. She would have to set off for Stirling first thing in the morning to fetch her luggage.

Pale light was beginning to show at the edges of the curtains when she fell into a heavy sleep from which she was awakened only by the sound of a breakfast tray being placed on the table beside her bed. As her eyes fell on the dainty white and gold clock beside her bed, she was appalled to see how late it was.

A pretty young girl with thick, inky-black curling hair, dressed in a flowered overall was pulling the curtains open, and as Miranda exclaimed at the lateness of the hour, she said cheerfully, 'Oh, that's all right! Mr Graham said you were to sleep on as long as you liked—especially as you were disturbed last night.'

As Miranda sat up in bed the first things her eye fell on were the red suitcase and matching travelling bag in vinyl, her luggage for her trip about Scotland. 'Where did those come from?' she asked in amazement.

'Oh, Mr Graham had Andy Blair fetch them from Stirling first thing this morning,' the girl told her airily.

'Andy Blair?' Miranda repeated.

'Yes, he's the new man, the one who's in charge of the caravans. But you'd better take your breakfast, hadn't you, before it grows cold.'

As Miranda poured tea she was thinking that Graham Lairdlaw had wasted no time in getting her established at Drumdarrow. In spite of his apparently easy-going ways he had placed her in a position where it would be difficult for her to back out of accepting the job. But Graham Lairdlaw would find he had met his match, she decided, as she snapped a piece of toast with determination. She would take herself *and* her luggage off, if necessary.

To the girl she said nothing of this: instead, she inquired, 'Caravans? I didn't know there were any at Drumdarrow.'

'Oh, this is a new thing,' the girl told her. 'It's one of Mr Graham's latest ideas. This is the first year we've had them, and very successful it's been too! But then Mr Graham's wonderful at thinking up ideas to make money for Drumdarrow. Andy Blair manages them for him. He's an experienced man.'

It was so plain that the girl was repeating something she had heard that Miranda could hardly keep from smiling.

She looked up to see the girl regarding her thoughtfully, and said, 'I didn't see you last night.'

'No, I'm Ida Morressy. I live in the village and only come in during the day to help out.' She paused for a moment, and then went on with a rush, 'I heard there was a great to-do in the middle of the night. Screams

35

and all that. Maybe you thought you saw a ghost.'

'Nothing of the sort!' Miranda told her crisply. 'A log of wood fell out of the fire and set the hearthrug alight. I hurt my ankle yesterday evening, and wasn't very well able to put it out on my own, so——'

'So Mr Graham came in and gave you a hand,' Ida giggled.

'Well, yes——' Miranda said reluctantly. It was plain that her screams in the night had been heard by others as well as Graham.

'He's frightfully romantic, isn't he? Every girl in the village is in love with him.' Ida sighed luxuriously.

'Is that so?' Miranda returned tightly, thinking that this attitude was all very well for a romantic young girl. But she had every intention of hanging on tightly to common sense.

When Ida had gone, Miranda lost no time in preparing for work. She put her foot down gingerly on the floor and was delighted to find that it gave only a slight twinge. She would be able to get about all right, provided she remembered to take things slowly.

She unpacked her luggage, put on a snowy fresh blouse and a swinging skirt of checks in palest yellow and blue and made her way carefully down stairs.

'Oh, there you are! And how is your ankle today?' the housekeeper greeted her. 'But there, I can see it's much better. You were lucky it turned out to be only a slight sprain.'

'I can manage all right, provided I don't hurry,' Miranda told her. 'In fact, I'd like to get to work right away. Did Mr Lairdlaw leave any instructions for me?'

'Well, he told me to give you the keys to the display tables,' Mrs Gilmore told her, 'And to show you the room where you're to work.'

Together they went upstairs again, and Mrs Gilmore showed Miranda into one of the most beautiful rooms she had ever seen. On three sides it was lit by long lancet windows, the lozenge panes leaded: tapestries covered the walls and in an oriel window was a table at which she was to work.

'Oh, how beautiful!' Miranda cried. 'It will be wonderful to spend my time here.'

'Yes, everyone who sees it admires it,' the housekeeper agreed complacently. 'It's Miss Shona's favourite room too.'

'Oh, is that so?' said Miranda. 'She's artistic, perhaps.'

'Well, not artistic exactly,' Mrs Gilmore said doubtfully. 'Not that she's knowledgeable about art, I mean, but Miss Shona loves everything beautiful. You should see the lovely things she has, everything of the very finest and best. And as pretty as a picture with her soft little blonde curls and her big blue eyes, and with a nature to match—all kindness; and so considerate of other people's feelings. None of that off-hand manner that so many of today's young people have!'

Miranda felt a twinge of embarrassment as she heard this description of Shona. What a contrast there would be between them, she was thinking, because she was aware that in many ways she was not what Mrs Gilmore would designate a 'sweet' person. She was too forthright, too given to stating plainly her attitude towards things!

'It's amazing how well she hits it off with Mr Graham,' the housekeeper went on, 'because he's not the easiest person in the world to get along with. But then it's hard to quarrel with Miss Shona! In fact, if she has a fault at all, it's that she's a bit too tender-hearted. A cold look or a sharp word pierces her to the heart. You have to be very careful about what you say, because she's so sensitive. Sometimes I don't know how she manages to put up with Mrs Gregg, for a more difficult person——' The housekeeper left her remark unfinished, and pursed her lips. 'Yet, in her own way she's fond of Mr Graham and I think she'd like Miss Shona to marry him.'

'And does she—care for him?' Miranda inquired.

'Yes, indeed,' the housekeeper returned. 'Miss Shona is simply crazy about him. But he——' Mrs Gilmore shook her head dubiously. 'Well, no one can tell with Mr Graham. He might care deeply, or he might just like her—in a cousinly sort of way, if you know what I mean. No one can tell with Mr Graham. He passes things off with a joke, you see, while all the time he may be feeling deeply.'

That was true, about Graham, Miranda was thinking when eventually Mrs Gilmore left her. It would be difficult to assess his true feelings. Under his teasing and lighthearted manner there was a complex character, too subtle to be analysed.

Next instant she had picked up the keys and was hurrying towards the display tables in the long gallery. It was none of her business what Graham Lairdlaw's character was like, she was telling herself sharply, as she inserted the key in the lock.

CHAPTER THREE

MIRANDA was examining a tiny, gold-framed mirror from the days of George the Third when a large hand reached over her shoulder and closed over it and Graham's voice said, 'So this is how you spend your time, gazing into your reflection in the mirror, like the queen in *Snow White*!' As Miranda swung around with a gasp, he went on, 'And what do you read in the strange, mysterious little face in the mirror?'

'What do you mean?' she demanded with more asperity than she intended. 'There's nothing mysterious about me!'

'Look again,' he commanded. 'Now tell me what you see.'

Miranda studied her reflection doubtfully. What was she truly like? she wondered. She was not plain, she knew that. But she doubted if she possessed any of the mystery he had mentioned. Was he quietly mocking her?

She was unprepared for his change of tone as he said, 'I think I could get to like you, Miranda Lorimer, if your character were at all in keeping with your appearance.'

Miranda put the mirror down so hastily that it clattered on the surface of the table. 'Now what do you mean by that?' she demanded, as she examined it to make sure no damage had been done.

'I mean that instead of velvety brown eyes you should have eyes of steely blue: instead of a mass of soft brown hair, yours should be worn in a severe bun: instead of a little heart-shaped face, yours should be a strong-featured one, with a large nose and jutting chin.'

'Why—why——' But Miranda was at a loss for words.

In the silence he picked up a Tudor thumb ring and pushed it upon her finger, where it twisted and quickly fell off.

'Rather large for an engagement ring,' he remarked. 'But tell me, if it *were* an engagement ring, what kind of man would you be engaged to, do you think?'

'The kind of men I like are serious, responsible types,' she informed him. 'And if you don't care for my character, let me tell you that I don't care for yours either.'

She spoke resolutely, but as she did so, she was thinking that the type of girl he would care for would be a gentle, utterly feminine sort of girl—a girl like Shona Townsend.

But then it was easy for a girl who had been brought up in the lap of luxury by a doting aunt to be tender and clinging. Her own story had been very different. There had been no cosseting for her! And now that her education was completed, she would have to make sure of holding a job.

'It's amazing to find we're in agreement on any point—even that we're not each other's types!' And Graham went out laughing.

But Miranda as she resumed her polishing of the gold frame of the mirror was feeling distinctly ruffled. This man had the power of upsetting all her preconceived notions. A complex, difficult man to understand, but a man with a fascination that was dangerous. She would not allow herself to fall victim to it, she determined.

After lunch, which she had alone, she found the afternoon passing swiftly as she examined the display-cases minutely, making notes of those articles that were in need of attention.

It was while she was passing one of the long embrasured windows that she heard a car approach along the drive. It was only then that she realised how silent and solitary her surroundings seemed without the clatter and chatter of tourists.

Glad of the diversion, she crossed to one of the windows, knelt on the window seat and looked down.

An enormous, old-fashioned-looking car was sweeping in a wide arc towards the main door. Out of it stepped a tall, imposing-looking woman, dressed in Harris tweeds and a no-nonsense hat that only seemed to accentuate the stern horsiness of her features.

But it was the girl who came from behind the driving-wheel and followed her who attracted Miranda's attention. This must be Shona Townsend, and her aunt, the redoubtable Mrs Gregg, Miranda thought.

Mrs Gilmore had been right, because Shona was one of the prettiest girls Miranda had ever seen: ash-blonde curls fell on either side of a perfectly formed face: even from her perch Miranda could see that her eyes were widely-set and guileless: on one side of her curls she wore a russet velvet tam-o'-shanter with a matching waistcoat over a dress of hunter's green. She had the subtle air of assurance that perfect taste and grooming can convey, and Miranda stared at her fascinated.

She saw Graham run down the steps towards them, and Shona impulsively fling her arms about his neck and kiss him.

Mrs Gregg, on the other hand, proffered a cheek with an air of rigid formality. It was not surprising, Miranda thought, that Mrs Gilmore dreaded her arrival.

They disappeared into the house and Miranda returned to her task with a feeling of strange discontent. Instead of being satisfied that Graham Lairdlaw had indeed been speaking the truth concerning their arrival, she realised that she was disappointed in some way, now that they were safely under the roof. It would mean that her status in the house would be quite altered. From now on Graham would probably be engrossed in entertaining his visitors—and in particular the charming Shona, who so obviously was attracted by him. She herself would, from now on, be simply the girl who had turned out to be conveniently useful. Tucked away in her room off the gallery, her existence would be almost forgotten. She would no doubt, she thought a little crossly, be taken for granted.

She worked for an hour or two, then locked the cases and, after a last look round, went to her bedroom. She switched on the lights. Outside the countryside was bathed in the soft, smoky rays of autumn. It would be a slightly frosty night, she knew, as she stood at the windows for a long moment before drawing the heavy curtains.

She was wondering dismally how she would spend the evening, when Mrs Gilmore knocked and entered the room.

'Mr Graham wants you to come down to tea,' she announced. 'I'd say Mrs Gregg is anxious to have a look at you,' she added. 'As soon as your name was brought up, nothing would do her but you'd be introduced.'

The housekeeper sounded worried and abstracted and Miranda guessed that Graham's aunt had already managed to ruffle her feathers.

For a moment Miranda hesitated. She would dearly have liked to refuse the invitation, but, apart from feeling a decided longing for a refreshing cup of tea, she realised that Mrs Gregg was the type of woman to regard a polite refusal as a sign of weakness on her part. Well, she would be in for a surprise, Miranda assured herself, and unconsciously her small face hardened determinedly.

'If I were you I'd take no notice of anything personal Mrs Gregg might say,' Mrs Gilmore suggested hurriedly. 'She's used to speaking her mind and doesn't care what she says when she's in one of her moods. And of course,' Mrs Gilmore added with a sigh, 'there's no use crossing her, for she's always the winner!'

It was a sort of warning not to cross Graham's aunt, or it might cost her her new job, Miranda realised. Well, much as she liked the prospect of remaining at beautiful, Drumdarrow Castle she had no intention of acting the subservient employee to Mrs Gregg. After all, Graham Lairdlaw himself was demanding enough, she told herself crossly.

'I'll just change my dress and go down,' Miranda assured the housekeeper.

'You won't be long? She doesn't like being kept waiting,' Mrs Gilmore said worriedly, as she hurried away.

Miranda decided to wear an uncrushable dress of jersey in a paisley design of turquoise, tangerine and sapphire blue. It was a favourite of hers, but so far she had worn it only twice, as she had always seemed to be keeping it for those special occasions which so seldom turned up. But now was the time to wear it, she decided. After all, Shona would probably be dressed in something wildly expensive, she was thinking as she combed her hair smoothly back and fastened it with a tangerine velvet bow.

When she was ready, she considered herself carefully in the mirror, thinking that she certainly didn't look like the nondescript governess brought down from the gloom of the attics to be surveyed by the company, and the idea gave her a certain satisfaction, for she had the idea that Graham Lairdlaw would be looking forward with a hint of malicious enjoyment to her first encounter with his dragon aunt. He had probably encouraged Mrs Gregg to request her presence in the drawing-room. Yes, from what she had seen of Graham Lairdlaw he would no doubt be anticipating her ignominious defeat. Well, the Laird of Drumdarrow would be in for a surprise, she told herself firmly, as with a last glance in the mirror, she went downstairs.

But as she approached the drawing-room floor she felt a sharp twinge of apprehension. Should she fall foul of these two new arrivals Graham, she knew, would not come to her rescue, because he had made it perfectly plain by his attitude that he considered her much too self-confident. He would be only too pleased were she to be vanquished in the coming interview— because that was really what it amounted to. The invitation to join the tea-table was to be the scene of a trial of strength between Mrs Gregg and herself, with Graham the amused onlooker.

For a moment she was tempted to turn and retrace

her steps, and to send an excuse by Mrs Gilmore, but she knew it would be taken by Graham as a confession of weakness.

She squared her shoulders and holding her head high walked slowly into the huge drawing-room: instantly, she was the focus of attention of the group by the chimneypiece.

Graham was standing before the fire, his hands behind his back, his dark figure outlined against the white marble of the chimney surround: Shona, in a dress of delicate, icy pink, reclined like a weary kitten in a wing-backed armchair, and Mrs Gregg presided behind a laden tea-table.

As Miranda slowly made her way towards them, Mrs Gregg laid down a silver tea-pot and surveyed her with open curiosity, and Miranda, feeling her cheeks grow pink, was furious at her own betrayal of her embarrassment.

'And this is Miss Lorimer, whom I was telling you about,' Graham was saying blandly. 'She has agreed to take care of the collection.'

'So I gathered,' Mrs Gregg said acidly. Her voice was deep and slightly hoarse and her bulbous eyes met Miranda's with a look of cold appraisal before Graham turned and introduced her to Shona.

Seen at close quarters, it was clear that Shona was even prettier than she had seemed at a distance, because now it could be seen that the widely-spaced eyes were of a gentian blue: she could have been the heroine of an old Scottish tale, Miranda thought fleetingly.

She smiled at Miranda, showing tiny, almost childlike teeth. 'Graham has been saying all sorts of lovely things about you, Miss Lorimer,' she said softly. 'It

45

makes me feel so useless. But then I was never clever with my hands. In fact, I'm afraid I was a complete dunce at school!'

'Nonsense, Shona!' Mrs Gregg broke in abruptly. 'It's simply that a girl as pretty as you are doesn't have to learn a skill, like any Tom, Dick, or Harry. And now, Miss Lorimer,' she continued when Miranda was seated and supplied with tea and sandwiches, 'you must tell us all about yourself. I must confess I was astounded when Graham told me the story of your arrival. I mean, it seems so extraordinary! After all, you were only one of the sightseers, and now, here you are, established in the Castle in a sort of semi-official position, as far as I can make out. You must realise yourself how unconventional the whole affair appears!'

Miranda felt her heart beat rapidly with anger. It was only too clear what Mrs Gregg was hinting at, and an angry retort arose to her lips. But, as she laid down her cup, she happened to catch Graham's eye. He was regarding her with an air of bland inquiry, but she detected the little gleam of mischief. She tilted her head and returned Mrs Gregg's protuberant gaze coolly.

'Actually, I had no intention of remaining. I agreed only when Mr Lairdlaw told me that you and your niece were coming to stay.'

For a moment there was silence as Mrs Gregg digested this.

'In other words you decided to use my arrival to satisfy the proprieties.' Mrs Gregg laughed shortly. 'Am I supposed to be flattered that you consider me a suitable chaperon?'

'I should imagine that, with your manners, you'd

make an excellent chaperon,' Miranda returned quietly, and heard a smothered laugh come from Graham's direction.

He tried to disguise it by pretending to choke on a piece of chocolate cake. But his aunt had not been deceived: her weather-beaten face turned a dull purple and for a moment she was at a loss for words.

Then, recovering herself, she said quickly, 'Shona dear, won't you have a piece of Madeira cake. It's really delicious, and you've eaten hardly anything.'

'Auntie dear, I must think of my figure,' Shona said, in her plaintive, little-girl voice. 'I'd get as stout as Mrs Gilmore and Graham wouldn't like me any more.'

'But I like Mrs Gilmore,' Graham told her solemnly.

'Oh, you know what I mean,' Shona said a little petulantly.

'Of course he does, my dear,' Mrs Gregg put in soothingly. 'He's only teasing you! And what's more, Graham, I've come to the conclusion that you take a delight in springing unwelcome surprises on me: first it was Andy Blair and now it's Miss—Miss Lorimer.'

'But, my dear aunt,' Graham told her, 'you know I needed someone to manage the caravans. And Andy has proved a most excellent choice. All summer we've been packed out, and soon the climbers will be along. He's certainly proved to be extraordinarily competent.'

'And so handsome!' Shona put in.

Andy Blair! The name was familiar, and Miranda recalled what she had heard about him. She already knew that he was in charge of the caravans and it was he whom Graham had instructed to drive to Stirling that morning to fetch her luggage from the hotel.

'Handsome, indeed! You're much too impression-able, Shona,' Mrs Gregg sniffed. 'And I can't see what that has to do with whether he's competent or not. But to get back to the subject, Graham, I still don't know why you engaged someone to take care of the collection. It has been perfectly all right up till now without professional attention.'

'That's just where we've been all wrong! We've been too complacent. It took Miranda's sharp eye to see that some of the most important pieces have been badly neglected.'

'And suppose they were!' his aunt put in sharply. 'What is it to do with you? After all, Drumdarrow belongs to Nigel and there's no reason why you should put yourself out over his possessions, while he idles his time away in Italy.'

Miranda had been aware that during this speech a subtle change had come over Graham's attitude: no longer was he amused by his aunt's eccentricities.

His hazel eyes narrowed and his voice had a gritting edge as he said, 'My cousin Nigel is an old and a sick man; he is forced to live in Italy. He cannot live at Drumdarrow, but he trusts me to look out for his interests and I intend to do so, so let's have no more about it!'

Then, as though to underline the inflexibility of his determination, he added in a totally changed voice, 'You should really sample some of this chocolate cake, Aunt. Mrs Gilmore will be so disappointed if you don't.'

'Nonsense!' Mrs Gregg returned, but her voice was noticeably less strident and Miranda got the distinct impression that she had been badly shaken by Graham's uncompromising stand. 'I am well aware that Mrs Gilmore dislikes me intensely. She knows I keep a sharp eye on things and can spot any signs of neglect. But then women like her always take advantage of a bachelor and let things slide!'

'I see nothing sliding about here,' Graham said, his lazy good-humour restored.

'You know perfectly well what I mean!' his aunt grumbled. 'Why, I could write my name in the dust on the hall table!'

'It's a pity she wasn't equally negligent where the gallery floor is concerned,' Graham observed. 'It was there that Miranda slipped and hurt her ankle.'

'Oh, did you hurt your foot?' Shona inquired sympathetically. 'I noticed when you came in that you were limping a bit, but I didn't like to remark on it, in case you were sensitive about it.'

'I'm not at all sensitive,' Miranda smiled. 'Anyway, it was only a slight sprain and it's nearly better now.'

'What's this about slipping on the gallery floor?' Mrs Gregg put in sharply.

'Simply, my dear Aunt, that Miranda became so engrossed in our collection that she didn't notice the time passing; then, realising she was going to miss her bus, she bolted along the gallery and fell on the highly polished floor.'

'Really, how extraordinary!' Mrs Gregg said.

'Extraordinary in what way?' Graham inquired. 'That Mrs Gilmore had had the floor polished, or that Miranda slipped?'

'It was a slip that turned out to be extremely convenient for Miss Lorimer. After all, it has procured for her a job eminently suited to her qualifications.'

'Speaking of your qualifications, I'm sure you'll need tools,' Graham remarked to Miranda.

She admitted that she would need cleaning materials, and some tools, but nothing very elaborate as there was no soldering or enamelling to be done.

'In that case you may as well get them tomorrow,' he remarked. 'I'll be driving into Glasgow and I could pick you up somewhere afterwards and drive you home. But be ready bright and early in the morning, because I want to make an early start.'

He sounded casual, but there could be no mistaking the fact that she was receiving an order.

His tone was very different when he turned to Shona, Miranda noticed, feeling a flicker of resentment.

'Would you care to come along?' he asked gently. 'But I don't think you'd find it very interesting. I've business to attend to, and Miranda will have her shopping to do. You'd probably be pretty bored.'

Miranda saw Shona hesitate for an instant, and in the pause Esther Gregg put in very decisively, 'Don't be ridiculous, Graham! This is not at all the sort of expedition she would enjoy. After all, you'll be there on business! You'll be unable to devote much time to Shona. Then again, you'll have Miss Lorimer with you.'

Esther Gregg's attitude was only too plain! She felt that a covert insult had been offered to her niece by asking her to make one of a party with a stranger—and one whom she evidently considered a scheming interloper.

'If you think I'd be bored, there's no point in my going, is there?' Shona said sulkily. 'You certainly don't make it sound the sort of thing I'd enjoy. What am I to do with myself while you're going about your tiresome business? And Miss Lorimer will be busy too, so I shouldn't even have her to speak to.'

'You're right,' he agreed. 'I don't think it would be a particularly good idea for you to come.'

At this Shona's gentian-blue eyes filled with tears. 'So you think I shouldn't come! Well, I don't believe in forcing myself on anyone. I know when I'm not wanted.'

'Now Shona, don't be unreasonable!' Graham said easily.

'Shona's not being unreasonable,' Esther Gregg put in sharply. 'It's just that she's an extremely sensitive girl, and I think it's time you realised that, Graham, and made allowances.'

There was a grimness in Graham's expression as he regarded his aunt. But his voice was without inflection as he said lightly, 'But I do make allowances—especially in your case, Aunt Esther!'

For a moment Mrs Gregg looked disconcerted; she made a great business of refilling her teacup.

As though unaware that his dart had struck home, Graham spoke to Shona. 'One of these days you and I shall go on an interesting trip together—just the two of us alone. Would you like that?'

Shona gave him her wonderful candid, childlike smile. 'That would be wonderful, Graham,' she said eagerly.

'All right, it's a date,' he agreed. 'And now, Miranda,' he added briskly, 'remember I want to set off after breakfast, so don't dawdle—there's a good girl.'

There had been such a change in his manner when he spoke to her that Miranda felt angrily that he was making it all too clear she had no choice in the matter, and felt an angry retort rise to her lips. But she forced

51

it back.

She must remember that, although she had been invited down to tea, she was not a guest in the house—just a person whose skills were useful in the Castle at that moment.

There was an awkward silence that seemed to lengthen embarrassingly.

Mrs Gregg gazed grimly through one of the windows, as though dissociating herself from the whole matter.

This was the point at which she was expected to make her departure, Miranda knew.

'I must be getting back to my work,' she said awkwardly, getting to her feet.

She walked as steadily as she could towards the door, but winced as she felt a momentary twinge in her ankle.

'Oh, your poor foot is hurting, isn't it?' Shona exclaimed sympathetically. 'You must let me help you upstairs, Miranda.'

And before Miranda could protest, Shona had uncurled herself from her chair, and crossing the floor had tucked her small hand under Miranda's arm.

In a friendly intimacy that Miranda found heartwarming, Shona guided her upstairs and left her only when they had arrived outside the door of her room.

As she was about to turn away, she said with a conspiratorial smile, 'Be sure not to let Graham overwork you! Oh, I know he can be devastatingly attractive when he wants to, but he can be perfectly horrid at times!' The large kittenish eyes regarded Miranda solemnly. 'You must take my word for that, because you see I think I know him better than anyone else.'

Then, turning, she walked swiftly away.

As she went into her room, Miranda was thinking that Mrs Gilmore had been right—Shona was that very rare combination, a girl who was as kind and thoughtful as she was beautiful. It would be wonderful to have a girl of her own age in the house, someone to laugh and gossip with, and Shona had shown every sign of wanting to form a friendship, Miranda thought happily.

Perhaps, for once, Shona would not allow her own attitude to be dictated by that martinet of an aunt, for Miranda had the distinct impression that Esther Gregg would thoroughly disapprove of their friendship.

CHAPTER FOUR

On the following morning Miranda rose early. An autumn frost encased the countryside in a silvery gleam and every blade of grass seemed outlined stiffly under a translucent coating of white enamel.

She felt a fierce determination to be first to appear at breakfast. She would be coldly polite to Graham, she decided, demonstrating that she was well aware that she was not a guest at Drumdarrow.

But when she did reach the dining-room, she discovered that Graham was already established at the table, munching toast.

He looked up and grinned, as she entered the room. 'Don't look so disappointed,' he said admonishingly. 'I have the distinct feeling that you hoped to be first on the field.'

'I'm only obeying instructions: you made a point that you wanted to make an early start,' she reminded him coldly, as she helped herself to porridge and joined him at the table.

'Need you take me so literally?' he asked. 'Aunt Esther and Shona won't make their appearance for some time yet.'

Miranda shook sugar over her porridge with calm deliberation. She felt coolly in command of the situation. Probably, she decided, Graham was disappointed that her punctuality had deprived him of the opportunity of playing the heavy-handed employer.

'You've employed me; you gave me your instructions, and naturally I obeyed them to the letter,' she told him.

She was aware that he was watching her closely, but managed to keep her features set in what she hoped was an expression of prim efficiency.

'You're a provocative little pixie, aren't you?' he remarked quietly. 'Sitting there, all smug and virtuous!'

Miranda who had been helping herself to a spoonful of porridge, almost choked at this unexpected attack.

'And must you put sugar on your porridge?' he inquired. 'We use salt in this part of the country, you know.'

Miranda rallied sufficiently to say, 'No, I didn't know. And I don't see why I shouldn't use sugar if I want to.'

'Well, it doesn't seem to have added any sweetness to your disposition,' he told her.

'You didn't engage me for my sweetness of character, I presume,' she retorted. 'You thought I'd be useful when you decided to employ me. I don't imagine you cared particularly what I was like.'

'And you resent that! Is that it?'

'Resent what?' Miranda countered. Had she given away more than she intended? she wondered uneasily.

'Don't pretend you don't know what I mean! You feel I'm taking you too much for granted, isn't that it? You're a pretty girl, in spite of the fact that you've a horrid disposition. I expect you're used to being rather spoilt by men, and have no intention of being taken lightly.'

'That's not true!' Miranda exploded in sudden anger. 'You're deliberately misunderstanding my attitude. I consider you my boss—someone who pays my salary, nothing more or less!'

'Good!' he replied equably. 'Now that that's settled we know exactly where we stand, and can drop the subject. I expect you'll enjoy the drive, at any rate. We'll go by Callander and Stirling and you can catch a glimpse of the Castle once more. Did you visit it, by the way?'

When she shook her head, he went on, 'Pity! It's very old indeed, dating back to the early days of Scottish history. By the way,' he added, as Miranda helped herself to tea and toast and a small portion of scrambled egg, 'you'd better eat more than that! We're hearty eaters in these parts and the sooner you get into our Scottish ways, the better. Anyway, you're far too skinny,' he informed her with the candour that Miranda found particularly disconcerting.

'I don't expect I'll need to get into your Scottish ways,' she told him. 'After all, I shan't be here long.'

'So you don't feel you'll be happy here at Drumdarrow? Is that it?'

She regarded him dubiously. Was the remark simply a draw to assess her attitude? 'I don't know yet, but I'll give it a trial,' she replied cautiously.

Afterwards, as she got into the car beside him, she was feeling decidedly ruffled. It was difficult to adopt any particular attitude towards Graham Lairdlaw because it was impossible to tell with his sudden mercurial changes of front when he was serious and when he was quietly mocking.

But soon the beauty of the morning smoothed her ruffled plumage. As the sun brightened, the mists began to disperse and to float away like diaphanous chiffon scarves and the countryside in all its myriad glorious autumn colours lay revealed. The rowan trees were hung with clusters of scarlet berries and their leaves too were turning a fiery crimson. Tall oaks, golden-leaved birch and dark sage green hollies clothed the hillsides and through the woods, hidden here and there by banks of saffron bracken, little burns like narrow silver ribbons cascaded from rocky ledges and gurgled along the roadsides in deep mossy channels.

At one point a deer dashed from the woods and bounded across the road, causing Graham to brake sharply and swerve on the narrow winding road. In the ditches Miranda saw rosy hips dangling like polished gems on bare, black, arching branches.

As they approached Stirling the sight of the Castle, seeming to float high on a cloud of mist like a castle in a fairy tale, made her give an involuntary gasp of delight.

'So Stirling Castle is one thing in Scotland you approve of,' he said with a smile.

'It's wonderful,' she replied. 'As if the very walls

were steeped in Scottish history!'

'Yes, extremely old! It goes back to an ancient Pictish settlement, although parts of it date from different times. All the great names of Scotland are associated with it—Wallace, Bruce, Mary Queen of Scots, Bonnie Prince Charlie! In fact, Mary Queen of Scots's boudoir can still be seen with her initials cut above one of the windows.'

Miranda listened eagerly and he shot her a quizzical sideways glance.

'I guessed you'd be interested in that morsel of history.'

'Did you? But why did you think I'd be particularly interested in that?'

'Because I'm convinced that under that prim, reserved exterior there beats a romantic heart.'

But she refused to be drawn. 'I don't see how Mary Queen of Scots can really have visited all the places that are associated with her,' she said.

He gave a burst of sudden laughter. 'You are a sceptical little character, aren't you? Or rather, you're giving a very good imitation of being one! I'd say that underneath all that show of being hardboiled there is a very soft core.'

'You're completely mistaken,' she told him with acerbity. 'And, as far as Mary Queen of Scots is concerned, from the portraits I've seen of her I don't even believe that she was particularly beautiful.'

'Now that I find hard to believe,' he teased. 'Of course she didn't have modern beauty. But only a person with a heart of stone could resist her charm. No, I don't believe a word you say.'

'You'll soon find out that you're mistaken about me,' she told him, trying to sound coolly indifferent.

But she had the feeling that she had not been particularly convincing.

'Well—time will tell,' he agreed. 'But I do believe I've got the measure of you, Miranda.'

And now they were driving through the outskirts of Glasgow and Miranda, as she glimpsed well-built but grimy buildings, found that Graham had fallen silent. His mind, she was aware, was engrossed in whatever business had brought him into town. He had been talking, just to pass the time; to relieve the boredom of the journey, and now that his mind was on his own affairs he had almost forgotten her existence.

She too remained silent until they drew up at the door of a jeweller's suppliers in the commercial part of the town. Here he accompanied her in and arranged that anything she selected should be charged to him. 'Just send the bill along to Drumdarrow Castle,' he instructed the assistant. Then, turning to Miranda, he said, 'We'll collect the parcels on the way back. When you've finished here we'll meet and have lunch.' Here, he mentioned the name of one of Glasgow's premier hotels.

Miranda found that her purchases were quickly made. She took a taxi into the centre of the town and began to stroll about admiring the displays in the exclusive shops. In Buchanan Street she viewed the beautiful tweeds and rich expensive shoes, handbags and gloves; handsome luggage that just seemed to beg to be taken on a luxury cruise; scents from France; luxury items in onyx, gold, marble and silver.

As she drew near the hotel he had mentioned, she stopped to gaze into the windows of a big booksellers. Books had always fascinated her, and she loved reading. Now, her eye was caught by a thin volume of poetry, *The Lady of the Lake* by Sir Walter Scott. But she hesitated about going in to purchase it. She glanced at her watch and saw that she would have to choose between her book and being late for her appointment with Graham—and that, of course, was unthinkable.

'I can see by the expression on your face that you're intent on squandering your money,' Graham's voice spoke behind her.

'Not squandering it,' Miranda corrected. 'I've always been led to believe that books are a good investment.'

'But hardly a girl's best friend,' he grinned. 'And what exactly is it that you're looking at so intently? Surely not that paperback with the extremely lurid cover?'

Miranda laughed. 'No, I wanted to get that copy of *The Lady of the Lake*, but I didn't want to be late for lunch. I love Scott's poetry, and that edition doesn't look too expensive.'

'Aha, so your secret's out! You like romantic poetry! Well, now that I'm here, you may as well have your heart's desire.'

He marched into the shop, Miranda following at his heels.

As they stood at the counter, waiting to be served, he said, 'I didn't know any of you English read Scott nowadays.'

'Well, I haven't read much of his poetry since I was at school,' she admitted. 'I read bits of *The Lady of the Lake* then, and I liked it, but I didn't understand it very well. I think I'd enjoy it better now. It's set in the Trossachs, isn't it?'

'Yes, that's right,' he agreed. 'Thousands of Americans come to make a sort of pilgrimage around the places he mentions in his poems.'

When the assistant came up, Graham requested a copy of the book, but when he saw it was rather a commonplace, inexpensively bound volume, he said, 'This is not what I had in mind. I want something rather special.'

The assistant glanced towards Miranda and with a faint smile disappeared, and returned with an exquisitely bound slim volume in gilt red morocco.

'Just what I had in mind,' Graham assured the assistant. 'But don't bother to wrap it.' He paid for it, and slipped it into his pocket.

As Miranda accompanied him out of the shop, she felt a growing sense of embarrassment. The cost of the exquisite volume had left her breathless. Why had she spoken so quickly and so thoughtlessly? Had he felt perhaps that there was some onus on him to present her with it? Certainly had she been on her own she would have been perfectly satisfied with a cheap copy.

As they went into the spacious, old-fashioned hotel with its broad carpeted foyer and its enormous Victorian dining-room with tables swathed in spotless linen, she felt gauche and awkward.

But Graham appeared not to notice. He made a few desultory remarks that needed no answers, and ordered a meal of simple but exquisitely cooked foods. A light wine was served with it and gradually Miranda found herself growing more relaxed and confident.

'I—I hope you didn't think that I wanted such an expensive volume? I'd have been perfectly satisfied with something much simpler,' she said, as, towards the end of the meal, he passed it across the table to her.

'Nonsense!' he replied. 'We can't have Scott presented in a shabby manner. Poetry especially, it seems to me, calls for a rich binding; something handsome to handle and to put on one's shelves. Besides, I enjoyed buying it and I hope you'll enjoy having it.'

'It's a wonderful present,' she said a little shlyly. 'And now will you do something more for me?'

'Certainly, if I can,' he smiled.

'Will you inscribe it?' she asked.

'If you're sure that's what you really want,' he returned. His speckled eyes were, for once, grave as they gazed into hers.

'It will help me to remember Drumdarrow Castle—and especially today.'

'But, more important, will it remind you of me?'

Miranda looked away, afraid to meet the intent gaze of those observant eyes, in case he should realise how much this moment meant to her.

He took out a pen and quickly scribbled on the flyleaf.

Miranda drew it slowly towards her and read, 'To Miranda from Graham Lairdlaw' in his broad, sprawling script, flowing and bold and somehow expressive of the man. For a moment she held it in her hands, wondering at the delight she felt in this exquisite present, then she opened her bag and carefully slipped it in.

Afterwards, when they had collected Miranda's purchases, they drove north by the shore of Loch Lomond, where the little islands in the great lake were tufted with a riot of autumn colours and seemed to glide on the still, enchanted waters.

As Miranda gazed at the beauty of the scene before her, she involuntarily murmured the words of the famous Jacobite song, 'The bonnie, bonnie banks of Loch Lomond.'

'It's strange, but it's only when you see it,' she said, 'that you realise how true the words of the song are. It *is* bonnie.'

'Yes, but it's rather a sad song, isn't it? Remember those other lines:

'But me and my true love
Will never meet again
By the bonnie, bonnie banks of Loch Lomond.

But then most beautiful things have a certain element of sadness. Don't you agree?'

As Miranda gazed where the trees dipped their crimson and gold foliage to the water's edge, she thought how right he was. It was beautiful, but strangely poignant.

'But why should it be like that?' she exclaimed, her heart in revolt.

'Life is like that,' he said in his slow, deep voice. 'You're young and hopeful, and it's right that you should be, but in a very few years you'll find that all this sadness is a part of living, and a very important part too.'

Miranda glanced at him, thinking how complex he was, and feeling a little inadequate too. He was not a man whom she would ever find easy to understand. This was a mood he would reveal only in rare moments and she felt privileged to see a side of his character which, she felt instinctively, he concealed from Shona with her childlike naïveté.

On the other hand, it was clear that he loved Shona with a tender, almost avuncular affection. His manner towards her had a special, almost indulgent quality,

Miranda had noticed. Did this mean that he considered Shona a very special sort of person, or did it simply mean that he felt she was too self-absorbed and frivolous to be able to appreciate and understand the deeper side of his nature?

The thought that he had revealed to her a facet of his character that he would never show to Shona made Miranda's heart suffuse with warmth. So he looked upon her as someone to whom he could confide his thoughts! But why should she feel such pleasure at the realisation? she wondered. Was it because deep down she hoped that to her, and to her alone, he would make such heartfelt remarks? On the other hand, she reminded herself, it may have been simply the fact that she had been by his side during a passing sombre moment, a moment of sadness from which he would take care to shield kittenish and vulnerable Shona.

How difficult and complicated life was, she was thinking as they turned through the great gates of Drumdarrow and the castle loomed ahead around the bend in the drive, its turrets outlined against the sky.

As they got out of the car she gave a little shiver as a cold breeze swept across the grass and rustled the trees, and the piles of rusty oak leaves that had gathered around the boles turned and twisted in the air. Life could be sharp and bitter as well as sweet and beautiful!

But inside the house all was warmth and comfort.

They found Shona and Esther cosily ensconced in a small sitting-room.

'I had Ida put a light to the fire here in the parlour,' Esther announced as they came in. 'The afternoon turned quite chilly. And I always think central heating is never the same when one really wants to toast one-self. I hope you've no objection, Graham.'

'And a lot of use it would be, if I did object,' Graham returned as he dumped the parcel containing Miranda's purchases on a table.

He had quite discarded his former mood of sombre introspection. His voice was bantering and held that faint overtone of irony which was so habitual to him.

Shona, seated on the hearthrug, a book in her hand, regarded them owlishly over a pair of enormous, brown-rimmed glasses which merely served to emphasise the petiteness of her face, and the dainty modelling of her small childlike nose.

'You look very engrossed,' Graham remarked, crossing the room and looking over her shoulder, his finger-tips caressing the soft ash-blonde curls that clustered about her neck.

'I've been reading this book about the haunted houses of Scotland,' Shona announced importantly, 'and I don't see Drumdarrow included. Now why is that, Graham?'

'Really, what a morbid idea!' sighed Esther. 'Of course Drumdarrow is not included! It's not haunted, you see.'

'Don't be too sure of that,' laughed Graham. 'Only recently I heard the most extraordinary noises in the middle of the night; the sound of a maiden screaming in distress, and the crackle of flames.'

Here his eyes met Miranda's in a teasing smile.

Shona's eyes grew wide. 'Did you really?'

'Screams! Terrible screams, I assure you,' he repeated solemnly.

'Oh, don't, Graham!' Shona begged. 'You're making me nervous. I'll be afraid to go to bed tonight.

I shan't shut an eye!'

'Nonsense!' Esther said sturdily. 'Can't you see he's joking? And I do wish you'd stop it, Graham! You know how sensitive Shona is!'

'Are you really joking?' Shona appealed to him.

'Of course!' he assured her.

'Then what was it all about? The screams, and fires, I mean.'

'The explanation is very simple. It happened the first night Miranda was here.'

'Miranda! But what on earth would it have to do with her?' asked Shona, her eyes opening wide.

'There happened to be a big log fire in her room and one of them fell out on the hearthrug. Luckily I happened to be on the spot, and when I had done my knight-to-the-rescue act calm reigned once again at Drumdarrow.'

'But how on earth did you *know* it had fallen out?' Shona persisted.

'Oh, don't get the wrong impression!' he laughed. 'As you will remember, Miranda had sprained her ankle. She wasn't able to go upstairs, so I——'

'I know,' Shona put in eagerly, 'So you carried her up. But how like you, Graham! You're always so kind and considerate. But do go on! I mean, about the screams and the fire in the middle of the night. It's quite exciting.'

He sighed. 'Really, Shona, need we go into all this?' he protested.

'But I want to know.' Shona looked up at him, her small mouth mulish.

'And so do I!' Esther said with emphasis.

'But there's nothing to tell! Before I left the room I threw some logs on, because the night was rather frosty. Later, one of them fell out and set fire to the hearthrug. That's all.'

'And you ran in and rescued her, just like a knight in shining armour,' Shona said, with a little trill of laughter.

'Well, I couldn't let Drumdarrow burn to the ground, could I?' Graham demanded dryly.

It was at this point that Miranda, growing exasperated with this exchange, said sharply, 'I suppose it wouldn't have mattered if I had burned, provided the castle was saved?'

'You'd only just arrived, remember,' he returned gravely. 'We hadn't learned to know and love you then.'

'Really, Graham, you do talk such utter nonsense!' Shona said, biting her lip with her small pearly teeth.

Miranda, glad to escape from the scene, picked up the parcel saying, 'I'd better arrange these things, so that I'll be able to begin work first thing in the morning.'

Upstairs in her workroom, she carefully dusted her table, took out her new copy of *The Lady of the Lake*, and laid it in a place of prominence, where she could gaze at it, then, smiling at herself, she began to open the parcel and to lay out her equipment in a workmanlike way.

She had barely completed her task when, to her surprise, there was the sound of the heavy door creaking open and Shona came in.

'You must tell me all about your day in Glasgow,' she said, and drew up a heavy carved chair to the table.

She leaned her elbows on the table and looked up at Miranda guilelessly. 'I'm simply gasping to know *every-*

thing. After you'd gone I was sorry I hadn't agreed to go along. It was so boring here, and Aunt Esther does nag so! And anyway, it's always such fun being out with Graham. He can make everything, even the simplest excursion, exciting and fun. You feel that too, don't you? I could see in your face when you came in that you'd had a simply marvellous time. Somehow you looked different—radiant.'

'Different?' Miranda echoed, feeling slightly uncomfortable. Yes, she had thoroughly enjoyed her excursion with Graham. But did it so clearly show?

'Nothing very exciting happened,' Miranda said casually. 'We drove back by Loch Lomond, and of course it was simply beautiful. So many places don't come up to expectation. But Loch Lomond was just as I imagined it would be——'

She stopped because it was only too plain that Shona was paying not the slightest attention.

While she had been speaking, the girl had idly reached out for the copy of Scott's poem, her white fingers had riffled through the tissue-thin pages and as she came to the inscription on the flyleaf she paused with a gasp.

'To Miranda, from Graham Lairdlaw!' Her voice had lost its soft, almost lisping quality and was now sharp and inquiring. 'Do you mean that Graham *gave* you this?'

'Well, yes,' Miranda found herself faltering, feeling almost guilty.

'It's not one of the books from the library, is it?' Shona pursued.

'No, it's not from the library,' Miranda was forced to agree. 'It's quite new.'

'Oh!' Shona's delicately traced eyebrows arched.

'So today, when you went to Glasgow, he actually bought you this book and inscribed it? Is that what happened?'

'Not exactly,' said Miranda. 'It didn't happen quite that way. I mean, he didn't stop at a shop and say he'd buy me a book. In fact, it was more my idea, if you know what I mean.'

'In other words, you asked him to buy you this?'

'It wasn't like that at all,' Miranda protested, feeling herself being dragged further and further into a morass of misunderstanding. 'It just happened that I was looking into the window of a booksellers and he happened to come along and asked me what I was looking at, and——'

'I think I see,' Shona said slowly. 'It's quite typical of Graham. He loves giving little gifts to people. Every time he goes on holiday he brings back a gift for Mrs Gilmore. I don't know why I asked you these things,' she added with a little disclaiming laugh. 'I'm sure you thought me perfectly horrid. After all, it's nothing but a book of poetry! It's not at all like the sort of present Graham buys me when we're out together. No dusty old books, I can assure you! I must show you what he bought me on my last birthday. I'm sure you'd love to see it. It's really exquisite. It's a brooch made in the form of a basket of flowers, the basket made of gold filigree, and the blossoms composed of emeralds, diamonds and sapphires.'

'Yes, of course I'd love to see it,' Miranda said hurriedly. And, in an effort to placate the girl, she added, 'You're the kind of person who wouldn't be interested in books. I'm sure you'd prefer jewellery.'

As she said the words, she was appalled to see Shona jump to her feet, her delicate skin flushing angrily.

'Really, I see no reason why you should deliberately be rude! I've shown you nothing but kindness since you came, and yet you say a horrid, snide thing like that!'

'But I didn't mean anything!' Miranda protested, dismayed at the girl's reaction. 'All I said was——'

'You're making out that I'm horrid and greedy! A sort of gold-digger! You said I was the sort of girl who wouldn't care for the present of a book, but would prefer jewellery!'

'But I didn't mean it *that* way!' Miranda protested, appalled by this interpretation of her remark.

'Of course you meant it,' Shona returned.

'But what I meant to say was that you're so pretty that jewels would look well on you!'

But Shona was not to be placated. Her rosebud mouth puckered ominously. 'Oh, how could you be so unkind! And I did so want to be friends with you!'

And, bursting into tears, Shona rushed from the room.

Miranda sank down on a chair, utterly confused and dismayed at Shona's extraordinary accusation. Added to her distress was the guilty feeling that she had been tactless and awkward. She had meant to make a compliment, but how unfortunately she had worded it! Now there was nothing to be done but to wait until Shona had calmed down and again offer an olive branch.

It was chilly in the large room and she decided to go along to her room and put on something warmer.

She walked to the door and was on the point of switching out the lights when she stopped. Quite clearly she could hear Shona's plaintive tones and the deep, soothing murmur of Graham's voice.

'Oh, she was so horrid! Horrid!' Shona was sobbing.

Again Miranda could hear Graham speak, but it was impossible to distinguish what he said, and as she stood irresolutely in the doorway, Shona's voice said loudly, 'I shan't tell you exactly what she said, because I'm not a troublemaker, but you can take my word, she was rude to me. Rude, and unkind—and ungrateful too, because I offered her friendship. I know, Graham, that you don't understand how I feel about these things, because you don't realise how sensitive I am. But I feel things dreadfully. It was such a wounding thing to say, and I feel completely shattered.'

In the silence that followed, Miranda stepped out into the corridor, her heart thumping uncomfortably.

There framed in a cluster of lights where the main corridor branched off were Graham and Shona, her small curly head resting on his shoulder. His hand was gently smoothing her hair.

Miranda re-entered her workroom, and taking the book placed it in the back of one of the drawers in the table.

That was where it would remain until the end of her stay at Drumdarrow, she decided. Suddenly she knew that she had been about to imbue this slight token with a significance far beyond anything Graham had intended. She must in future take care not to allow herself a dream for which there was not the slightest foundation.

CHAPTER FIVE

ON the following morning as Miranda worked in her room off the gallery, she was still turning over in her mind the contretemps of the previous evening.

The more she thought over her remark to Shona the more gauche and awkward it seemed. It had not been meant maliciously: but how was Shona to know that? It would be so easy to interpret it as being gratuitously insulting. But her main consideration was how Graham Lairdlaw was reacting to Shona's complaint. She wondered uneasily if he believed that her remark had been made with the deliberate intention of wounding Shona. As she had not seen him since his encounter with the tearful girl in the corridor, she had no way of assessing his attitude.

This was partly due to the fact that she had felt unable to face him at dinner on the previous evening; on the pretext of doing a very special piece of work that could not be interrupted, she had managed to have Ida bring her something on a tray to the workroom, where she had put up a great pretence of being busy until quite late.

It had been different that morning at breakfast. She had gone down early with the deliberate intention of facing the music, but there had been no one there. She had breakfasted in solitary state and had been told by Ida that Graham had already gone off on business about the estate. Shona and Esther were having theirs later in their rooms.

Gradually as the morning passed and she became engrossed in her work, the problem slipped from her mind, and she was completely absorbed when the door opened and in came Ida with a tray.

'Is it lunch time already?' Miranda asked, her heart sinking at the thought that she was so deeply in disgrace that she had not even been asked to join the family at lunch.

Without answering, Ida came and peered at her work. 'What on earth is that?' she asked, gazing in distaste at an early nineteenth-century silver button which Miranda was examining.

'It's a silver button,' Miranda told her, 'but it badly needs cleaning.'

'Oh, I hate those old-fashioned bits of jewellery—they're so dull!' Ida remarked.

'This will be bright enough when it's polished,' Miranda smiled. 'It's just that the silver is badly tarnished.'

'I'll never get to like it,' Ida told her decisively. 'I hate old-fashioned things. Now the jewellery I like is the sort of present Mr Graham buys for Miss Shona, really lovely things, all brand new, and straight out of the jeweller's shop. Yes, I don't half envy her,' Ida sighed. 'To be so pretty and to have a man like Mr Graham buying expensive presents for her! But there, you'd better eat your lunch before it grows cold! You're having it in solitary state today,' Ida giggled, planking the tray in front of Miranda and removing the covers.

'The others have driven into Stirling and they're going to have lunch there. And I'm glad to see the back of that Mrs Gregg, I can tell you; it's nothing but, "Have you done this, Ida?" or, "Have you done that, Ida?" until I could scream. But when the cat's away, the mice will play—at least that's the way the saying goes! I'm going to take things easy while she's gone. I'll be busy enough when she comes back, goodness knows. Why don't you do the same?' she asked. 'You haven't as much as put your nose over the door since you arrived. You should take a walk out after lunch. Your ankle's a lot better, and a breath of air would do you all the good in the world.'

Miranda forbore to inform Ida that the reason she looked rather off colour was not due to lack of fresh air but rather to the nagging worry that Graham Lairdlaw might already be considering her dismissal.

'Perhaps, when I'm finished for the day, I'll take a walk,' she told Ida.

When the girl had gone, she picked disconsolately at the delicious and daintily served food that Mrs Gilmore had sent up. Her conversation with Ida had brought back to her very clearly the difficulties she had got herself into, and suddenly she became aware how quickly her attitude had changed towards her job. At the beginning it had simply been a way of filling in time until she found a permanent position. But now she was aware of how terribly she wanted to keep this job, and dreaded the thought of being sent away from Drumdarrow. Was it because she wanted to stay on and finish the work she had begun, she asked herself, or was it not rather that she could not face the prospect of never again seeing Graham Lairdlaw?

She pushed away her tray and resolutely returned to her work.

But now she found herself unable to keep her thoughts from Graham's possible reaction to Shona's complaints. If she didn't get out into the fresh air for a while she would scream! she told herself.

She got to her feet, collected her tools and cleaning

73

materials and put them away in the deep drawer of the table. Then she took the button, now glowing with a bright silvery gleam, and went into the gallery and replaced it carefully in its special spot in one of the display tables. Then, locking the table carefully, she took the key and replaced it in the worn tapestry bag that she kept as a sort of holdall for various odds and ends. The bag she put in the bottom of her suitcase, then locked it. At least Graham Lairdlaw would not be able to accuse her of carelessness!

Then, drawing a brush rapidly through her brown hair and applying a light touch of lipstick, she threw over her shoulders an anorak in a soft shade of jade green, then slipped downstairs and left the house by one of the side doors.

It was a wonderfully mild autumn afternoon and she walked slowly along, occasionally drawing her feet through the little drifts of yellow birch leaves that lay in piles of fairy gold.

She limped only very slightly now, she noticed with relief, and she was glad to think that soon she would be able to get back into her usual swift, athletic stride. It would be wonderful to walk through these lovely pathways, the wind blowing through her hair, or battling against the gales of autumn. Then she stopped herself with the thought that she was visualising late autumn days that she would probably never see here at Drumdarrow. Doubtless her fate was already sealed. This might well be her only walk through the beautiful Castle grounds.

She followed a winding path, bordered by saffron-tinted bracken, that led downwards to where she could see the narrow silvery ribbon of a river gleaming through the trunks of trees. Here she was able to make her way along a broad pathway running parallel to the water. Soon this widened, and she saw that, set at intervals were pretty chalets, each established in a grove of trees looking on to the water, and surrounded by well-kept gardens where begonias, chrysanthemums, dahlias and late roses were in bloom.

They were so quaint and unexpected that she stood and examined them curiously.

Each was a perfect little replica of a Swiss chalet, rustic and fitting unobtrusively into the general background of woods and bracken. As she walked past she could see that most of them were occupied: a narrow stream of blue smoke rising in the still air, reminding her of gingerbread houses in a fairy-tale.

She came to one before which stood a tall slender man: he was handsome, without being particularly distinguished, and in fact he had a frowning, discontented expression that gave his features an insipid look.

He walked down the short path to the gate and as she came level with him, to her surprise, he waved a greeting. 'You're Miss Lorimer, if I'm not mistaken, aren't you? May I introduce myself—Andy Blair. As fellow slaves perhaps we should get to know one another.'

As they shook hands, Miranda's surprise that he should know her seemed to strike him, because he said, 'There's no mystery about my knowing your identity. I'm afraid your slight limp gave you away. We've all heard about your accident and everyone knows that you're now in charge of the collection. May I flatter myself that you've heard of me?'

'I know you manage the chalets,' she smiled.

'That's right,' he nodded. 'Tell me, what do you

think of them?'

She could see that, in spite of his disgruntled air, he was proud of them, and anxious for her approbation.

'I was admiring them as I came along,' she told him sincerely. 'They're so beautifully situated and fit so perfectly into the surrounding countryside.'

'Yes, and they're very comfortable too,' he told her. 'A great deal of trouble has been taken to make them as luxurious as possible. Would you care to see one?'

'Yes, I'd like that,' Miranda returned eagerly.

At least it would help to pass away part of the afternoon, she was thinking.

'Each chalet has its own particular colour scheme,' he told her as he unlocked the door.

Off a small sitting-room, charmingly decorated in primrose yellow and silver, was a bedroom in the same colour-scheme: fluffy blankets were piled on the twin beds and were matched by the terry-towelling curtains at the casement windows. Both rooms had silver-grey fitted carpets that toned with the walls and cushions and gave a dainty springlike atmosphere to the tiny house. The kitchen, small and compact as it was, was supplied with gleaming equipment and shining ceramic dishes: yellow and silver tiles covered the floor.

'It's like something out of a fairy-tale, so small, yet so perfect!' Miranda exclaimed in admiration. 'I shouldn't be at all surprised if Goldilocks walked in.'

Andy Blair's look of repressed resentment gave way to a grudging smile. 'They're all the same as far as accommodation goes: only the colour-schemes vary. I take a great deal of care that everything is kept in apple-pie order: as soon as anything gets the least bit shabby it's renewed immediately. But then Graham Lairdlaw's a pretty exacting boss—as perhaps you've already discovered.' Then he added bitterly, 'But then he's king of the castle, isn't he?'

He waited, as though expecting a reply, and when Miranda, uncomfortable at the unconcealed bitterness of his tones, remained silent, he added, 'This chalet is vacant. You wouldn't by any chance be considering it, would you?'

She stared at him in astonishment. 'You mean, rent it?'

'Possibly you had that in mind when you strolled in this direction.'

'But why on earth should I? I'm staying at the Castle.'

'That's the very reason why I assumed you might be in search of more homely accommodation. For one thing, neither Shona nor that aunt of hers will welcome a pretty girl as a fixture at Drumdarrow. You've probably found that you're decidedly unwelcome—at least, as far as Shona is concerned.'

'You're quite mistaken,' Miranda told him coldly.

She walked towards the door, determined not to listen to any further unpleasant insinuations, then paused a moment, overcome by curiosity. 'Why on earth should you think such a thing?'

'Because Shona is in love with Graham Lairdlaw and will make things as unpleasant as possible for you.'

'That's where you're mistaken,' she told him almost triumphantly. 'Shona has shown me nothing but friendship.'

His cold pale eyes watched her without expression. 'All right! Let's say you're so naïve that you really believe that Shona is your friend, what about Mrs Gregg? She's generally loathed in these parts. You're

77

not going to tell me she's been all sweetness and light since her arrival, are you, for I simply won't believe it. I've had too much experience of that old witch's interfering ways and waspish tongue.'

'She is rather difficult at times,' Miranda admitted, carefully choosing her words.

'Difficult!' he scoffed. 'How discreet you are, Miss Lorimer! To put it plainly, she's determined by hook or by crook to marry her niece off to Graham Laird-law, and she'll let nothing stand in her way.'

'I hardly see how that has anything to do with me,' Miranda returned, determined to put an end once and for all to the conversation. 'I've nothing to do with the family. I'm simply an employee of Graham Lairdlaw's and——'

'And no doubt, as with every girl who comes his way, he's managed to make you fall for him!'

As Miranda turned and walked swiftly down the narrow pathway, he called, 'Don't forget! If you ever feel the need of a place of your own, let me know and I'll fix things up for you.'

As she walked back towards the Castle Miranda was asking herself why she had allowed herself to become involved in such a distasteful conversation. She should have put a summary end to Andy Blair's vituperations. It was obvious he bore a grudge against Graham Lairdlaw and was determined to air it. There was also something treacherous about the man, she decided, and in future she would tread warily where he was concerned.

She continued her walk, feeling angry and flurried. Andy Blair, it was plain, was one of those embittered people who always see the most hateful side of people.

A mist was descending on the countryside as she

turned for home and the colours on the hills had darkened to heliotrope and rusty red. The sky was heavy behind Drumdarrow as she hastened along the drive.

When she reached the Castle she saw that the others had returned because the long, aged, scarred oak table in the hall was piled with a miscellaneous jumble of packages and boxes and Shona herself was running lightly upstairs in her outdoor clothes.

On an impulse, Miranda hurried towards the foot of the stairs, and raising her voice said in a rush, 'I'm sorry about last night, Shona. I honestly didn't mean to hurt you.'

Shona turned, her eyes wide in puzzlement. 'Sorry about what, Miranda?' she asked in her soft, almost childishly sweet voice.

'Oh—oh, about our discussion of the book—and—and about the jewellery, and——' Miranda mumbled, beginning to feel conscious that she was cutting a distinctly foolish figure. 'I'm—I'm afraid I upset you. You must have been upset, because you spoke to Graham about it.'

Slowly Shona came downstairs towards her. 'Upset?' she queried, evidently at a loss. 'I really don't know what on earth you're talking about, Miranda. Why shouldn't I talk to Graham? I tell him everything—that's why we get on so well together. We're completely at home with each other.'

She knitted her arched brows. 'But I can't remember telling him anything in particular last night.'

Miranda, completely at a loss, fell silent and wished she had not given way to that sudden impulse to make amends.

And Shona, as though dismissing the whole matter, said with sudden animation, 'But I must show you what Graham bought for me today!'

She snapped open her expensive leather bag, extracted a small velvet case and, opening it, showed Miranda a tiny brooch in the shape of a terrier formed of small sparkling diamonds.

'Isn't it terrific! A sort of memento of our drive today.'

'Yes, it's certainly lovely,' Miranda agreed, without any particular enthusiasm for the gaudy little trinket.

Apart from everything else, she was puzzled by the fact that Shona had forgotten so quickly their spat of the previous evening—especially when she had wept floods of tears in Graham's sympathetic arms.

'I'm just going up to change,' Shona went on animatedly. 'Then I'll come down and show you and Graham all the things I've bought. Aunt Esther's tired out and doesn't intend to stir from her room tonight, so we can get really cosy and discuss plans without her continually interfering.'

'Discuss plans?' Miranda echoed.

Shona gave her little trilling laugh. 'You poor dear! Of course you don't know what I'm talking about, do you? I keep forgetting you're new here and don't know our customs at Drumdarrow. Never mind, I'll explain it all to you when I've changed.'

And flashing Miranda one of her warm, guileless smiles, she turned and ran upstairs.

As Miranda continued across the hall she was feeling particularly dissatisfied. Somehow her apology had not had the result she had hoped for—that of putting her mind at rest. Instead, she was puzzled and confused by Shona's attitude.

Then, as a possible explanation struck her, she felt her spirits rise. It would be quite characteristic of

Shona to pretend she had forgotten the whole unpleasant affair, so that their relationship could be resumed on its former friendly basis. How right Mrs Gilmore had been, when she had said that Shona had a particularly sweet nature!

When she opened the door of the parlour she was met by the usual warm, welcoming glow from a piled log fire.

Graham was contentedly smoking his pipe, seated comfortably in one of the winged leather armchairs that stood on either side of the hearth.

He glanced at her as she entered. 'Well,' he remarked, 'it looks as if you've been taking the air. Your cheeks have quite a few roses. Let's hope you don't lose them all, working up there in that room.'

'Yes, I took a walk by the riverside and saw the chalets.'

'Did you? And what is your professional opinion of them?'

'They're simply beautiful,' Miranda said quickly. 'And so perfect in every way! They look bandbox-fresh.'

'Yes.' He knocked his pipe against the carved stone chimneypiece. 'I see that they're kept up to scratch! Even if I rub Andy Blair up the wrong way at times.'

In spite of the affability of his tone, Miranda thought she detected a certain reserve in his manner towards her. Perhaps Shona, good-hearted and feather-brained, might forget her complaint, but Graham Lairdlaw was of a different mettle. He was the sort of man who would not overlook the fact that one of his employees had apparently insulted a guest—especially such a cherished guest as Shona.

'I particularly liked the idea of having different

colour-schemes,' she pursued, feeling herself becoming bogged down in inanities.

'So Andy showed you through!' he commented.

She nodded. 'Yes. They're the sort of little fairy-tale houses that one longs to live in.'

Then she could have bitten her tongue, as she saw him raise his brows quizzically. 'Indeed! Then I'm afraid your wish will not be granted. I'd prefer you here on the spot.'

He didn't elaborate on this statement and Miranda wondered if he were quietly conveying to her that he had not yet proved her trustworthy and that he intended keeping a close eye on her until she had his complete confidence.

Her quick temper was on the point of boiling over in an angry retort when Shona pushed open the door, her arms piled high with boxes. Above them her eyes gleamed with excitement in her small, perfect face, and Miranda felt a little stab of envy as she saw that Shona was wearing a dress of gentian-blue Chinese silk; the skirt was accordion-pleated, and swayed and fanned out with every movement of her graceful figure.

Shona tumbled her load on to the deerskin rug in front of the fire and plumped herself down: sitting crosslegged in front of the pile, she began to tear off the wrappings of the boxes with all the happy absorption of a child eagerly opening her presents on Christmas morning.

Miranda saw that from his chair Graham was looking down at Shona's activities with an indulgent, protective expression.

Soon she was surrounded by a jumble of gaily coloured crackers, boxes of coloured balloons, paper hats and favours, and discarded packages and wrap-ping-paper.

She held up a frieze of witches riding on broom-sticks beneath a large yellow moon.

'This will look terrific strung across the hall, won't it, Graham?'

Graham nodded, his eyes smiling quizzically.

Shona gave a disgusted moue. 'Well, you aren't enthusiastic, are you?'

'As I shan't be there on the great day, I can hardly tell whether they'll go down well with your little guests.'

'Now you're being horrid and obstructive,' she accused. And, turning to Miranda, she asked, 'Do you think the children will like these?'

'I can see from Miranda's expression that she hasn't the slightest notion what you're talking about,' Graham laughed.

'Well, no,' Miranda had to admit. 'I'm a bit at sea. They're for a party, I suppose.'

'You suppose right! A Hallowe'en party, to be exact,' Graham told her. 'It's been held here for the village schoolchildren every year since my grand-father's time. It's become quite a tradition at Drum-darrow. Actually, I used to rather dread it—that is, until Shona arrived on the spot. She makes a terrific success of these affairs and the children look forward to it.'

'Yes, I do think I've a way with children,' Shona said seriously. 'Whereas you don't like them at all, Graham,' she accused.

'You're wrong,' he answered in mock indignation. 'It's simply that some of them can be pretty trying. Last year, for instance, they managed to get jelly and custard all over the floor.'

'They did get rather over-excited and carried away,' Shona confessed.

'Well, try to see it doesn't happen again,' he told her seriously. 'The floors of Drumdarrow are much too valuable to be used as a playground for a crowd of rowdy children.'

But Shona wasn't listening. 'You haven't told me yet Miranda what you think of the witches.'

'I wonder if they would frighten the children, especially the young ones,' Miranda said doubtfully.

Shona's face fell. 'Oh, but I think they'll simply love the witches! They're exactly the sort of thing that appeals to children! I remember, when I was a child, I liked things to be rather creepy at Hallowe'en —roasting chestnuts around the fire, and telling ghost-stories by candlelight. That's all part of the fun! Last year I arranged masks around the hall and touched them up with phosphorescent paint. Then we turned out the lights. The effect was wonderful. The children were thrilled. It seems they spoke about it for weeks afterwards.'

'Perhaps it accounts for the fact that the kids got over-excited and many assorted goodies found their way on to the floor,' Graham said dryly.

'Oh, you are an old spoilsport,' Shona remarked airily. Then, turning to Miranda, she said eagerly, 'Can you think of anything fresh? I'd like something new this year, but I seem to be out of ideas.'

'Yes, have you any suggestions?' Graham asked lazily.

'What about the traditional Hallowe'en pumpkin?' Miranda suggested. 'You know what I mean—hollowed out, with gaps cut out for the mouth and eyes, and a candle inside.'

'We grow pretty nearly everything at Drumdarrow, but I'm afraid we simply can't boast of pumpkins,' Graham smiled.

'Oh, what a pity!' Shona's face fell in disappointment. 'It would have been a splendid idea! I could have put them down the centre of the table, with tiny coloured lights inside.'

'Well, I'm afraid it's out! So sorry to disappoint you, madam, but I'm afraid we haven't any pumpkins in stock,' Graham said with an air of mock pomposity.

'Perhaps we could make them,' Miranda said tentatively.

'But how?' Shona asked hopefully.

'I'm sure I could devise a fairly good imitation of a pumpkin out of coloured paper, wire and glue. We could choose the colours that appeal to children; reds, blues, orange, green, or any colour you'd like.'

Shona's eyes shone. 'But what a splendid idea! They'll make a wonderful table decoration. Will you begin right away, Miranda?'

'But, my dear girl, you've lots of time until Hallowe'en. Why the rush?' Graham asked.

'Oh, but Miranda will have to do them between her work on the jewellery! She'll need plenty of time. You'll begin tomorrow, won't you, Miranda?' she asked coaxingly.

Miranda laughed. 'I'd need materials—wire, to shape the outline, and fixative and coloured paper.'

'Can't you go into Stirling tomorrow and get them?' Shona appealed.

Miranda smiled and glanced awkwardly across at Graham, who was regarding Shona quizzically.

'You know, Miranda has better things to do than to

trot off to Stirling for paper for pumpkins. She's doing important work on the collection that's of value to Drumdarrow.'

'Oh, drat Drumdarrow and the mouldy old collection!' Shona exclaimed, springing to her feet. 'You're an old grouch, Graham.'

She snatched up a glittering paper crown and placed it ceremoniously on his head and then, holding out her wide blue silken skirt by its sides like a great fan, made a deep courtesy. 'Now you're king of the castle,' she announced, 'and I, your humble subject, crave the favour that you'll allow Miranda to go into Stirling tomorrow. Pray grant my wish, Your Royal Highness.'

Miranda saw Graham looking down into the wide, kitten-like eyes that stared up at him so appealingly. The firelight cast golden shadows on the ash-blonde curls.

'When you put it that way,' he said softly, 'how can I refuse you?'

Shona gave a little crow of triumph. 'There, I knew you'd do it!' She turned animated to Miranda. 'Tomorrow you must start off immediately and get everything you need.' Her voice was no longer wheedling, but held a hint of imperiousness that was not lost on Miranda, and she felt a smouldering resentment that the girl had assumed so readily that she was prepared to throw up her work on the collection and obey her wishes by going on this ridiculous errand into Stirling. After all, it had not been with the prospect of acting as dogsbody to Shona that she had agreed to stay on at Drumdarrow.

But Shona, sublimely unaware of her reaction, was again engrossed in examining her purchases and chattering away inconsequently.

Miranda glanced up to find Graham's eyes fixed on her. Had he guessed at her reluctance, and the reason for it? she wondered.

'You've no objection to going, have you?' he asked quietly.

'No, of course not,' she replied, trying to keep resentment out of her voice. 'After all, you've given your permission, so there's no reason why I shouldn't.'

'I see.' He regarded her levelly. 'That's it, is it? You'll go because—"yours not to reason why." I'm sorry if you feel you're being made use of, Miranda. I'd had hopes that you and Shona would become friends, which naturally would have involved your not sticking inflexibly to your work. You're much too young to be stuck away in the gallery all day long. I'd hate to think I was responsible for making you into a sort of recluse. But now that this is arranged, I'll drive you into Stirling tomorrow.'

'Thanks, but I can easily go by bus,' Miranda replied shortly.

He regarded her with a sort of exasperated curiosity. 'You *are* an independent little character, aren't you? Do you know, I don't think I've ever met a girl so irritatingly pigheaded as you are. You haven't, by any chance, been crossed in love, have you?' His eyes crinkled at the corners with amusement.

He was making fun of her, she thought hotly, but decided to stand on her dignity.

'No, of course not,' she replied coolly. 'And, even if I had been, I should certainly not tell you.'

'Then what on earth makes you so unco-operative?'

She remained silent, evading his searching gaze.

Impossible to tell him how lonely and out of things she felt. Shona was right! She and Graham Lairdlaw understood each other and in their company she felt as if a great intangible barrier lay between Graham and herself and that nothing she could say or do would penetrate it.

Shona glanced up. 'What are you two so solemn about?' she asked.

'I'm just trying to let Miranda see that the sky won't fall down if she takes a day off work tomorrow and goes to Stirling.'

Shona sighed and shook her curls. 'Miranda's so sensible and conscientious: she makes me feel completely frivolous and useless.'

'Well, every household has room for one useless and frivolous female,' he said lightly, as he bent down and began to gather up the clutter of wrapping paper and empty boxes. 'We'd better get this cleared away before Mrs Gilmore blows us up,' he told Shona.

For a minute or two Miranda watched as, with her usual inconsequential chatter, Shona helped him put the room in order.

Deciding it was time she tactfully retired, Miranda muttered a few words of excuse and went upstairs, feeling sure that neither of them were even aware that she had left the room.

CHAPTER SIX

On the following morning Miranda found herself breakfasting in solitary state. It was only as she was finishing that Shona appeared.

She looked surprised when she saw that Miranda was alone. 'Now, where's Graham? I understood he was to drive you into Stirling this morning.'

'I'm going by bus,' said Miranda.

'But that's ridiculous. It has all been arranged. Anyway, the bus doesn't pass through the village until the afternoon. Graham hasn't been horrid to you, has he? I know, at times, he can be very despotic. But let me know if he's been bullying you and I'll make him apologise.'

Miranda felt somewhat irritated at Shona's calm assumption that she was in complete control of the situation, and was in a position to assure her that Graham Lairdlaw would obey her slightest whim.

'It was my decision,' she told Shona shortly. 'I prefer to go by bus.'

Shona laid down her spoon and gazed at Miranda in astonishment. 'But why? It doesn't make any sense. As I said, the bus doesn't go past until the afternoon. You'll have very little time to do your shopping. Why on earth are you taking this attitude? It's completely inexplicable to me why you wouldn't let Graham drive you.'

'I suppose it is difficult for you to understand me,' Miranda agreed dryly. 'You're a guest here and I'm simply an employee. We regard things from different angles. I don't want any favours from Graham Lairdlaw.'

'Oh, Miranda, you *are* unreasonable,' Shona protested. 'You're my friend, aren't you? Well then, why do you take this attitude? It sounds so horrid and cold and unfriendly, so you must never ever feel that way again.'

'I like to keep my independence,' Miranda said firmly. 'You've never worked in a house in which you were a complete stranger. Your experience of life is entirely different from mine.'

'Yes, I expect I am rather spoilt,' Shona agreed thoughtfully. 'Aunt Esther simply can't refuse me anything, and Graham—well——' she shrugged. 'He's willing to satisfy my smallest whim. I know he would let me have anything in the world I desired. As to the future!' She laughed a little self-consciously. 'Well, as you've probably gathered, it's pretty well assured.'

Yes, Miranda was thinking, she did indeed gather that Shona was conveying that it was perfectly plain that her future would be that of mistress of Drumdarrow.

Later, when she was in the workroom, Shona made her appearance.

'Oh, do give up that horrid, dismal old work,' she exclaimed. 'I've everything arranged. I've ordered a taxi. That means you can go right away. Anyway,' she added, as though anticipating a rejection, 'it will probably rain. It always does at the most unexpected times in this part of the country, so don't argue, there's a dear.'

As she spoke she took from the large patch-pocket of her dirndl skirt a handful of notes and placed them on the table in a haphazard jumble. 'That's to pay for the trip, and for the things you'll need.'

'The materials won't cost much,' Miranda told her.

'All the same,' Shona insisted, 'I've no intention that you should pay for them out of your own pocket. Now, don't be silly,' she added, as though anticipating further objections on Miranda's part. 'Every year Graham gives me carte blanche when it comes to the Hallowe'en party. So why on earth should you be stuffy and obstinate about it.'

Miranda smiled. 'All right. But I certainly shan't need all that.'

How typical it was of Shona, she was thinking, that she should have no idea what would be a reasonable amount of cash for such purchases.

Shona sighed resignedly. 'Oh, all right! But you are tiresome,' she grumbled, as she withdrew some notes and pushed them carelessly into her pocket. 'But you must take the rest. And do have a proper meal while you're there, splurge, with all the trimmings. If you don't, I'll be awfully cross.'

'You always get your own way, don't you?' Miranda smiled.

'Nearly always!' Shona replied complacently. 'But sometimes Graham can put on his imperious, Napoleonic mood, and then it's almost impossible to make him change his mind.'

Almost, but not quite impossible, Miranda thought wryly as she tidied away her tools when Shona had gone.

But as she replaced the Tudor ring she was working on in its place in the cabinet, she felt her spirits rise, and hurried off to her room to change.

From her windows she had a wonderful panoramic view of the clear blue sky and the autumn-shrouded countryside, a magical tapestry of orange, amber and Venetian red.

She slipped into a sleeveless dress of mimosa yellow, with matching coat, feeling a vague happy sense of anticipation that she found it hard to account for. Soon she was being wafted down the drive in a large old-fashioned taxi.

Arrived in Stirling, she slipped into a café for a cup of tea. Afterwards, it didn't take her long to make her purchases. And when she had tucked them into a plastic shopping bag on which was depicted a highly coloured version of Stirling Castle, she decided to do some window-shopping. Immediately her eye was caught by a tiny antique shop with a small, low window in which was displayed an assortment of knick-knacks: an odd brass candlestick with snuffers; a grimy crystal decanter; a little dusty wooden box that contained odd buttons with pretty designs; a lump of rock crystal that was obviously intended as a paperweight. Among the usual hodge-podge contained by this kind of shop Miranda's eye was caught by some small African figures. They were roughly carved in hardwood and she hesitated, wondering if it would be worth her time to price them. They would probably be quite expensive, she was thinking, hesitating doubtfully, when there was a sudden shower of rain.

This decided her.

The shower would probably not last long, and she would spend its duration examining the other fascinating knick-knacks that she could glimpse tucked away. She pushed open the door: a shallow step led into the shop and Miranda was greeted by a small, round, jolly-looking woman who was in complete contrast to her sombre surroundings.

Miranda was on the point of putting her query when her eye was caught by the sombre gleam of a black African mask that hung in the shadows in the back of the shop: it looked crude and barbaric and rather frightening, but Miranda immediately recognised its decorative qualities.

The stout lady noticed where her eye had wandered. She nodded benignly. 'It's quite frightening, isn't it? It's a real genuine African mask. I bought it with those other things.' She pointed to the figurines in the window, 'when old Colonel McGregor was selling up before he went to live in Glasgow with his niece. He has spent most of his life in Africa and brought these home with him. A lot of people in these parts go to Africa, you know.'

'It is rather gruesome,' Miranda admitted. 'But, all the same, I like it.'

The proprietress looked a little doubtful. 'Well, if you do you're one of the few who have taken a fancy to it. In fact, between you and me, if you really want it you may have it fairly cheap, because I simply can't get it off my hands.'

'I think it's the way it gleams that makes it seem so ferocious,' Miranda smiled.

'Yes, Colonel McGregor used to tell me that when the Africans were finished carving a piece of hardwood, they'd polish it with black-lead.'

'Well, it's certainly made it very effective,' Miranda remarked. 'I should certainly like to have it—if it's not too dear.'

Eager to dispose of it, the little woman named a most reasonable price and Miranda, feeling all the thrill of a bargain-hunter, popped it in beside her other purchases.

She spent an enjoyable ten minutes poking around among the other knick-knacks, some well beyond her purse, others almost valueless.

By the time she emerged, the rain had stopped and the autumn sun was again tentatively smiling on the rain-washed streets.

She was standing at the edge of the pavement, preparing to cross the road, when a car swept up and she found herself looking through the window at Graham Lairdlaw.

He rolled down the window and grinned at her derisively. 'So you didn't take the bus after all! Don't tell me the independent Miss Miranda Lorimer got out on to the road and thumbed a lift?'

'No, I didn't,' Miranda told him quickly. 'I came by taxi.'

He raised his eyebrows. 'Oh, did you indeed?'

'Yes, Shona insisted I take a taxi.'

He nodded. 'Yes, that's typical of Shona! She's always thinking of others.'

Miranda didn't answer. No doubt it had been a generous gesture; on the other hand, Shona was determined to get her own way. She had wanted the purchases made immediately and by hiring a taxi she had managed to see that her wishes were obeyed.

But Graham didn't seem to notice any lack of enthusiasm on Miranda's part. 'Have you done all your shopping?' he asked.

She nodded.

'Well, you've plenty of time before you, and it's a gorgeous day. Why don't you pop in and we could have a look at Stirling Castle? After all, you may not get the opportunity again.'

Miranda hesitated. She felt a happy excitement at

the idea, but was determined not to capitulate too easily.

'Don't miss this unique offer, madam,' Graham intoned. 'She who hesitates is lost—and by the way, I mean that,' he ended seriously. 'If you don't get in immediately I intend to sweep off and leave you to your unhappy fate.'

His tone was bantering, but Miranda had the feeling that he was fully determined to carry out his threat. She immediately abandoned her pose of haughty indifference and pulling open the door scrambled in beside him.

'Ah, that's better,' he said, as they drove off. 'You're actually smiling. I gather you like the idea of seeing Stirling Castle.'

Miranda nodded. 'Oh yes, it's the kind of thing I enjoy more than anything else.'

For the next two hours Miranda found herself thoroughly interested. Without Graham by her side she would have found the frowning buildings, set high on a crag, much too redolent of their violent history. She would also have been confused by the mixture in styles of architecture, and she was surprised at how well Graham knew his way about; he must have studied the castle and visited it many times, she realised.

He explained to her that at one time it had been merely a Pictish settlement. Then, through the centuries, fortresses and buildings had been added, making a jumble of different styles, some buttressed and ornamented with the hideous gargoyles of the Middle Ages; others simply great cavernous halls where soldiers had been housed. She gazed in awe at the Chapel of the Holy Rood where Mary Queen of

Scots had been crowned queen at the age of nine months.

She was intrigued by the amount of carved stone lions that abounded until Graham told her that in the courtyard a Stewart king had kept a captive lion.

'Quite a handy thing to have around!' he remarked idly. 'It probably helped to keep out unwanted guests.'

And later she was surprised at the vividness of the picture he conjured up when he described how the palace gardens had looked in medieval times; formal terraced walks edged with hedges of box, along which cranes and peacocks had strutted and gallants in rich jerkins edged with fur had strolled along the gravelled paths on warm summer evenings with their ladies of the Court dressed in their long kirtles and floating veils and wimples.

'I didn't know you'd be interested in that sort of thing,' she said a little wonderingly when they had finished their tour.

He looked amused. 'Aha, but then I'm full of surprises! What about another Scottish experience before we set off for home?'

'Actually, I'm a little tired,' Miranda confessed, visualising a museum full of Scottish relics.

'It's nothing cultural,' he assured her. 'I'm simply suggesting you sample a Scottish high tea.'

'Tea, in any form, would be welcome,' Miranda admitted. 'But what's the difference between an ordinary tea and a high one?'

'That's what you'll discover,' he told her mysteriously. 'I can assure you, you've never before experienced anything like it.'

Later on, she had to admit to herself that he was right, for she found herself sitting before a table laden with the most extraordinary mixture of foods. There was the usual tea; bread, butter, scones of every description and Scotland's delicious and elaborate cakes. Apart from these items there was a large bowl of sliced tomatoes; there were pickled onions, and sauces, sausage rolls and Scotch pies. These were preceded by a hot dish of fried sliced haggis and egg which Miranda found very tasty, but afterwards, as she gazed about the laden table, she said with some alarm, 'Surely we're not expected to eat all this?'

He laughed. 'No, you can make your selection. Personally, I think high tea is one of our most happy inventions.'

'All the same, I think it would take some getting used to,' Miranda remarked. 'It wouldn't do much for one's figure. Perhaps it's just as well I shan't be staying here long.'

She saw him glance at her fleetingly. 'Then you're looking forward to leaving us, is that it?'

'Oh no, of course not,' she replied hastily. 'It's wonderful to work in such beautiful surroundings. And then Shona has been so friendly! I expect,' she added with a little laugh, 'that when it comes time to go I'll find it hard to drag myself away.'

When he didn't answer, she glanced up to find his eyes fixed on her with a strange, questioning expression that confused and embarrassed her. She looked away, conscious that she was colouring like a gauche schoolgirl. 'It's time we were going,' she said hastily. 'I hadn't realised how tiring sightseeing can be.'

As they drove home in comparative silence, Miranda found herself nodding off in the heated car and Graham seemed wrapped in his own thoughts. Once he braked abruptly and startled her into wakefulness as a deer bounded from the woods and flashed across the road.

When they arrived at Drumdarrow there was no sign of Shona or her aunt, and as Miranda parted from Graham, she felt a sense of almost guilty relief. She had made such a point that morning of refusing Graham's offer of a lift and now she had spent the whole afternoon in his company. It was wonderful not to have to explain her change of front.

Her room was pleasantly warm because, to her delight, she found that Mrs Gilmore had had a crackling good fire lit.

She had slipped off her coat and was on the point of unpacking her purchases when there was a peremptory knocking on her door, and, without waiting for an answer, Esther Gregg marched in. She glanced around the room critically and then directed her gaze pointedly at the blazing fire.

'I see you make yourself comfortable,' she remarked acidly.

'Mrs Gilmore makes all the household arrangements,' Miranda said quietly.

Esther Gregg sniffed. 'That woman takes far too much on herself. She knows Graham's not the sort of man who interests himself in domestic affairs, so she does exactly as she pleases.'

'You mean you object to my having a fire in my room? Is that it?' Miranda inquired.

She was determined not to be intimidated by Esther Gregg, for she saw the light of battle in the older woman's eyes, and knew how easy it would be to succumb to her domineering manner.

'I think,' Esther said sharply, 'that it's time you realised that you are not a guest at Drumdarrow and are not entitled to a guest's privileges.'

'That isn't what you've come to say, is it, Mrs Gregg?' Miranda asked.

'No, it is not.' Esther Gregg replied brusquely. 'I want to discuss something of a great deal more importance.'

She strode across the room and took her stance before the chimneypiece, fixing Miranda with a cold and accusing eye.

Miranda sank down on the side of her bed with a sigh. She had the feeling that she was in for an extremely unpleasant session and, in spite of herself, she felt her heart beating rapidly with apprehension.

'I wonder,' Esther began abruptly, 'if you realise how unhappy you're making my niece?'

Miranda stared at her in bewilderment. 'Whatever do you mean?'

'Don't pretend to misunderstand me! You know perfectly well what I mean,' Esther replied sharply. 'I happened to be looking out of my window and saw you and Graham getting out of the car. Obviously you were together in Stirling. Oh, don't bother to deny it!'

'I've no intention of denying it! And I can't see what it has to do with you!' Miranda retorted.

Esther's lips tightened. 'Did you, or did you not, tell my niece that you were not going to allow Graham to drive you into Stirling today?'

It was true, Miranda was thinking. She had said that. And she wondered if she looked as uncomfortable as she felt.

'I believe,' Esther continued, 'that you told Shona you were too—independent—that's the word I think Shona told me you used—to avail yourself of Graham's offer, yet now I find you've been in his company until late this afternoon. This is quite a change of face, I think you must admit. Did you arrange with Graham to put on this little charade?'

'Charade?' Miranda echoed blankly.

'Don't pretend to misunderstand me! You know perfectly well what I mean,' Esther snorted impatiently. 'He offered you a lift, which you refused. It was all arranged to pull the wool over the eyes of my poor trusting niece.'

'How could you say such a thing!' Miranda exclaimed, outraged. 'Do you really believe I could do such a despicable thing?'

'I am hardly in a position to answer that, as I know nothing whatsoever about you,' Esther Gregg replied contemptuously. 'From what I gathered, it seems you wormed your way into Drumdarrow on the pretext that you'd missed your bus back to your hotel—a fairly simple thing to accomplish, I should imagine. According to yourself, you were so engrossed in the collection, you didn't notice time passing. It all sounds very fine, of course, but we've only your word for it.'

'And do you also think that I arranged to fall and hurt my ankle?' Miranda cried.

'As to that—' Esther glanced sceptically at Miranda's foot, 'it appears to me it healed remarkably quickly; so quickly, in fact, that one wonders if it was injured in the first place!'

It was true, Miranda had to admit to herself, that her ankle had mended in a short time. But why on earth should Esther assume that she had concocted an elaborate plan to—as she put it—to worm her way into Drumdarrow?

'If you do really believe this,' Miranda said quietly, 'I'd be interested to know what you imagine my motive was in carrying through such a scheme.'

'Your motive!' Esther replied with a short harsh laugh. 'That's fairly obvious! You had already discovered that Graham was single, and no doubt you thought that, once established in the Castle, you'd be able to influence him!'

'Influence Graham? He seems to me to be the last man in the world to be influenced!'

'Perhaps not in most things! But it would be different when it came to a girl with a pretty face, who knew how to play her cards properly.'

Miranda sighed. The conversation, she decided, had become too ludicrous to be taken seriously.

'And suppose all this is true, what on earth has it got to do with you?'

'It has a great deal to do with me,' Esther snapped. 'I'm not going to sit back and see my niece humiliated and made little of. I'm getting rather sick of hearing Graham singing your praises. How wonderful it was that you arrived here, just when the collection needed attention, etcetera, etcetera. Naturally Shona resents it! What girl wouldn't, when she's in love with a man? Not that I blame Graham! It's simply that he's rather tactless at times,' Esther pursued, 'but I know Shona feels hurt and neglected.'

Miranda found herself regarding the older woman with growing exasperation. It had filled her momentarily with a heart-warming glow when she had heard that Graham had been praising her, but her pleasure had immediately been dashed by the realisation that he had spoken of her in that way because her skills were useful as far as the collection was concerned.

'I'm sorry Shona feels that way,' she said coldly. 'But she's completely mistaken. If Graham takes the slightest interest in me it's solely from a business point of view.'

She could say this in all sincerity, and it was evident that Esther had detected the transparent honesty of her reply.

She remained silent for a moment, then said, 'If you're sincere in what you say, then why do you let things go on as they are at present?'

'And what do you suggest I do?' Miranda asked dryly.

'I suggest you leave the Castle and move into one of the chalets. According to Andy Blair at least one of them is vacant at the moment.'

Miranda was silent, too stunned to reply. Then she said angrily, 'Do you really think, Mrs Gregg, that I shall move out of Drumdarrow just because you have the ludicrous idea that I have designs on Graham Lairdlaw?'

'I'm not asking much of you,' Esther protested. 'And it would make things so much more pleasant all round. After all, I'm sure you don't want to make Shona unhappy. She must see how you force yourself upon Graham, although the dear girl's too loyal to admit it.'

'I'm sorry if Shona's unhappy, for she has really no cause to be,' said Miranda. 'But as to going to live in one of the chalets, that's completely out of the question.'

Mrs Gregg's eyes narrowed ominously. 'Is that your final answer?'

Suddenly Miranda felt weary of the whole ridiculous discussion. 'Yes. And now I'd better get on with my work, Mrs Gregg,' she said pointedly.

'If you're so engrossed in your work, it strikes me

you should be doing it, instead of gallivanting off on jaunts with Graham Lairdlaw,' Mrs Gregg snapped.

Then, leaving the room, she closed the door behind her with a resounding crash.

When she had gone, Miranda resumed her work, but somehow she felt a vague uneasiness. Esther Gregg was determined to marry her niece to Graham Lairdlaw and she had no intention of letting anyone stand in her way.

A few days later Miranda sat at her worktable, busily constructing the pumpkin lanterns.

She was surrounded by a jumble of wire, coloured paper, paint and paste when Graham walked in.

She glanced up in surprise. She knew that Esther and Shona had driven into Edinburgh on a shopping spree and had assumed that Graham would be busy for the whole day.

He wandered about the room without speaking, picking things up and laying them down in an abstracted manner. It was clear to Miranda that he felt himself at a loose end when Shona was away, and she didn't feel exactly flattered by this visitation.

Eventually he strolled towards the table and looked down at her work. 'So this is how you pass your time when my back is turned—making pumpkin lanterns!'

But Miranda refused to rise to the bait.

'Well, what do you think of them?' she asked complacently, holding up the first of her efforts.

It was a lantern of shiny orange-coloured paper. Apertures indicating eyes and mouth had been cut out so that the light would shine through them: there were sickle-shaped eyebrows made of black paper pasted on, and the mouth turned up at the corners in a wide grin. Altogether the effect was gay and festive, and Miranda had every reason to hope that the children would be delighted with her efforts.

He perched himself on the corner of her table and fingered the lantern. 'Don't tell me this has been evolved from wire, paper and some glue. How on earth did you manage it? I'm beginning to think you're quite a clever little person.'

'Thanks!' Miranda retorted crisply. 'I'm glad it's dawned on you at last.'

He wandered off towards the oriel window, so obviously bored that for once Miranda found herself rather nettled by his company. So he had nothing better to do than to visit her!

'Hello, what have we got here!' he exclaimed with a low whistle. And Miranda saw that his eyes were fixed upon the mask which she had hung up on the panelling to one side of the window.

She had polished it with black-lead in accordance with the hint the antique dealer had given her, and now it gleamed with sinister beauty from the shadows.

'Well, this is an ugly-looking customer!' Graham was exclaiming.

'Do you not like it?' Miranda asked quickly.

He regarded it thoughtfully. 'Yes, I like it. It's interesting and attractive too—in a weird sort of way—and very dramatic.'

What a strange man Graham was, Miranda was thinking, feeling a warm glow of pleasure in his appreciation of the mask. Somehow it was as if it were very important that he should like it! But she had not dared to hope that he would value it.

'It's yours, of course?' Graham queried.

'Yes, I saw it in a small antique shop in Stirling, and I couldn't resist it.'

'You couldn't resist it!' He echoed, coming back to the table to stand looking down at her. 'To think that a pretty little girl like you should have such strange tastes! But then I'm beginning to realise that you are rather out of the ordinary. Is it really true that you bought this the day we went to see Stirling Castle and that you didn't even mention it?'

'But why should I?' she parried.

'Perhaps it's because I thought you'd have told me your little adventures.'

'I didn't think it would interest you,' she said.

'It does interest me. In fact, everything about you interests me.'

'Even my buying an African mask?' she laughed a little shakily.

'Buying a mask like this is a very revealing thing!' he informed her. 'It tells quite a lot about you—about the sort of person you are. You should have mentioned it.'

'But how was I to know you're interested in African art?' she returned.

'Now you know,' he told her. 'We have this interest in common—another interest in common, by the way, which means that there are a number of things upon which we see eye to eye.'

At the thrill of delight his words gave her, Miranda looked up—only to feel a hardening of her heart as she saw the smile on his lips. He was only flirting with her because Shona was away for the day and he was bored, she thought resentfully. How clear was the resemblance to his ancestor, that Colin Lairdlaw whose portrait hung in the long gallery; Colin Lairdlaw, the man of many love affairs, the swashbuckler and charmer, who had enjoyed exerting his attractions.

She would not let her feelings carry her away, Miranda promised herself. How foolish she would be to let herself fall victim to Graham's wiles, when all the time he was only bored by Shona's absence. As soon as Shona returned, she herself would be relegated to her true position in his life—that of the little nonentity who spent her days tending to the furbishing of the collection; someone dusty and forgotten, like the antiques on which she spent her care.

So when, a few moments later, he invited her to join him in a walk in the grounds she immediately gave a sharp refusal.

'No, thank you,' she returned very decisively. 'When I've finished the pumpkin lanterns, I've plenty to do.'

'This is my work you're doing,' he remarked, 'and I say leave it.'

'I couldn't possibly,' she told him.

'You'll do as I say,' he retorted.

And, as she still hesitated, he pushed the lanterns to one side and pulled her to her feet.

Miranda stood indecisive for a moment, her feelings curiously mixed. She resented his high-handed behaviour, and yet felt glad that he had insisted. Perhaps, after all, he really did want her company! It would be wonderful to be walking through the autumn countryside with Graham, instead of spending the rest of the afternoon a prisoner in this silent room.

'I'd—I'd better fetch a coat,' she said, still undecided whether to yield, or to stick to her guns.

But he had read her mood.

'Oh no, you don't,' he told her. 'It's a mild day. You won't need a coat. Besides, I've the feeling that should I permit you to retire to your room, you've half a mind to shut yourself in there and not to emerge again for the rest of the day. Now, off we go!'

He took her by the arm and marched her to the door.

CHAPTER SEVEN

HE took her in a direction which she had not yet seen; through a beautiful little birch wood, where tiny golden leaves lay in piles upon the ground. Further on they came upon a group of rowan trees hung with glowing berries: and on, until they came down to the shore of a beautiful, still, silent lake on either side of which were autumn woods, their brilliant colouring reflected in the water, as in a mirror.

By the edge of the water was a little beach composed of beautifully coloured pebbles. With a little exclamation of delight Miranda stooped and picked up one of a beautiful deep pink shade.

'It was from pebbles like these that Prince Albert had a bracelet made for Queen Victoria,' Graham remarked when Miranda praised the beauty of the stones. 'It seems she was delighted with it. Strange to think that the woman who was later to be Empress of India should have taken pleasure in a pebble bracelet.'

'I'm sure she valued it more than any of her fabulous jewels,' Miranda said softly.

'What makes you say that?' he inquired.

'Because it was given to her by the man she loved,' Miranda told him.

'And does this mean that you would treasure such a thing, regardless of its value if it were given to you by the man you loved?' he asked.

'But of course,' she said.

A frown crossed his brows, and turning away, he picked up a flat stone and idly skimmed it across the water.

What was he thinking of? Miranda wondered, as her eyes followed the flight of the stone soaring and falling on its journey across the surface of the loch. Had her remark sounded like a covert criticism of Shona, who loved to receive expensive presents and who made no secret of the fact that their value was important to her? She bit her lip, regretting the remark.

He swung around and stood regarding her thoughtfully for a long moment and Miranda turned and began to climb a narrow path leading upwards through a little copse of slender trees. Graham followed her and in a few minutes they stood side by side in a grassy space in which were the ruins of a cottage and a single slender rowan tree.

In an attempt to return their conversation to the normal, Miranda remarked on the tree, hung with bright berries.

'It was probably planted by the young bride when she came to that house,' he remarked. 'At one time every household had one near the door to keep away the evil eye.'

Miranda stood gazing at the ruins of the little house. 'To think that a little family once lived here!' she remarked.

'Yes, no doubt it appeals to your romantic heart!' he remarked. 'If you would delight in a worthless bracelet, no doubt you're able to picture yourself living in one of these primitive but-and-bens. You think that you would be happy—provided you were with the man you loved.'

Miranda was silent. This was exactly her feelings, but she reminded herself that Graham's tastes were not for the simple and homely. He loved beautiful and exotic Shena with her expensive clothes and demanding tastes. It was clear that Graham was a man who was impatient of primitive, and earthy things.

So, denying the truth in her heart, she said defiantly, 'You're quite wrong about me. I simply can't visualise myself in surroundings like these. It wouldn't be the life for me.'

'So you believe that when poverty comes in the door, love flies out the window, is that it?'

'Exactly!' she announced very positively, although she knew that in her heart she wanted nothing so dearly as that she might find happiness with a man she could truly love—no matter how poor he might be.

Again he was regarding her thoughtfully. 'You know, Miranda, you're a very contradictory sort of person. Just when I think I'm beginning to understand you, you say something that directly goes against everything I know of you.'

Confused, Miranda made a show of glancing at her watch. 'It's time we were getting back to the house,' she said hurriedly.

As they turned towards the Castle Graham said little, and Miranda was conscious of the confusion of her thoughts. How wonderful it would be to walk by Graham's side and to feel free to say to him all that was in her heart! Never to have to pretend! Never to have to be defensive, or false to what she truly believed to be right and good! But always she would have to remember that, for her, there could be no future in allowing herself to fall under the spell of Graham Lairdlaw.

Graham reopened the conversation on a lighter note, and they were laughing as the woodland path ended and they emerged on the drive. At the same instant, the car bearing Esther and Shona passed.

The smile froze on Miranda's lips as the two women turned their heads and she saw the look of startled amazement that came into their faces. She could only stare after the car, while Graham waved affably.

But Miranda could not but feel that Shona and Esther had some cause for their startled reaction. After all, how did it appear to them? They had left that morning, while she had been immured in her workroom; they were returning to find her strolling in the grounds with the master of the house. Miranda had a curious feeling of guilt and self-reproach: it had been foolish to have accepted Graham's invitation. True, he had put it very forcibly! But, had she really been in earnest, she could have refused.

That evening Miranda was putting her things away for the day when Shona strolled into the workroom. She had changed into culotte trousers in black velvet with a shell-pink velvet jumper and looked cool and at her ease. It was very seldom Shona visited the workroom and Miranda waited tensely to discover what mood she was in.

Shona strolled across the room and stood looking down at the pumpkin lanterns.

'But these are simply wonderful!' she exclaimed enthusiastically. 'This one especially!' she indicated a lantern made of purple paper with fantastic peaked eyebrows in startling emerald green. 'The children will simply love these. How on earth do you achieve such effects?'

'Oh, they're not really difficult,' Miranda began, relieved to find that Shona was in a good humour. 'You make a frame of wire, and over that the paper is pasted. After that, the faces are up to yourself! But I agree with you, I think children like something a little bizarre—as long as it isn't too frightening, of course—and——'

She drew to a stop, as she looked up to find Shona regarding her, a frown on her pretty face. In the great gentian blue eyes was a hard stare, curious and calculating. It was clear that whatever Shona had come to discuss, it wasn't the construction of paper lanterns.

'Whose was the suggestion that you should go for a walk this afternoon, yours or Graham's?' she asked, her voice hard.

The change in her tone was so startling that Miranda found herself almost stammering as she replied. 'It was—was Graham's—of course!' Then steadying her voice, she added, 'why do you ask?'

'Because,' Shona answered tightly, 'I wasn't aware that he was paying you to spend the afternoons strolling about at your ease. On the other hand, if he invited you that's different, of course. Where did you go, by the way?'

'We went down to the loch,' Miranda replied.

'Dear me, how romantic! You certainly seemed to be getting along very well together as we drove past. What was the big joke?'

Miranda hesitated. At that moment she could not remember what they had been talking about at that particular moment. All she could remember was that there had been a wonderful rapport.

'Perhaps it was something too precious to be told,' Shona resumed.

'I—I just can't remember what we were talking about,' Miranda protested.

'That's strange! Most girls can remember what Graham says to them. He's that sort of man. But of course, if it's something you can't repeat to me——'

'It was nothing, really!' Miranda repeated.

'Well, whatever it was, it wasn't business you were discussing, that was clear,' Shona retorted. 'You weren't laughing over your work on the collection, I presume.'

'No. Really, Shona, it was only some silly joke. Nothing very special,' Miranda assured her.

'Well, you didn't go for a walk together without speaking about *something*,' Shona insisted.

'We looked at the ruins of the old cottage overlooking the loch,' Miranda assured her. 'We talked about that for a while.'

'Ruins of an old cottage?' Shona's eyebrows had risen. 'That's hardly engrossing! It was plain that it wasn't old cottages you were discussing when I saw you in the drive. You were both in hilarious form, that was clear. You're a lucky girl to be able to interest and amuse him so much, because Graham's not a man to be easily entertained.'

Miranda was silent. She felt rather guilty in spite of the fact that it had not been her fault. How would she have felt had she been in Shona's shoes? she was thinking. She had made up her mind so definitely not to poach on Shona's preserves, yet when Graham had persuaded her, she had weakly yielded, drawn by the lure of being in his company for a little while.

'Really, I think it's shameless, the way you make up to Graham,' Shona said sharply. 'I've spoken to Aunt Esther over and over about this, and she told me she has pointed it out to you, but it doesn't seem to have made any difference.'

Miranda stared at her unbelievingly.

So it was Shona who had instructed Esther to warn her off—and she had blamed Esther for this! It would have been more straightforward of Shona had she done this herself, instead of sheltering behind Esther.

However, as Shona continued, it was clear that she was no longer masking her attitude behind the pretence that it was Esther who disapproved of the growing friendship between her and Graham.

'In future just stick to your work,' Shona instructed. 'Remember, you're not a guest here! And don't get any ideas about Graham, because you're nothing to him—nothing!'

She swung on her heel and strode from the room. Miranda stared after her as the door swung to behind her.

That evening Miranda had her meal in her own room, but she felt too upset to eat. Over and over in her mind chased the scathing words Shona had said. Again and again she reviewed her own conduct. It seemed unfair that Shona should blame her. After all, it had not wholly been her fault, and——

Ida came in to take her tray and her face fell as she saw that the food had hardly been touched. 'Why, you've eaten hardly anything!' she exclaimed. 'And it was just the same downstairs this evening! Everyone in bad humour and hardly touching their food. I wonder what can be the matter!' Here Ida eyed Miranda knowingly. 'Mr Graham in a rare bad humour! Mrs Gregg as snappish as anything! And poor Miss Shona—well, anyone can see she'd been crying her eyes out.'

So the whole household knew that she had been out walking with Graham while Shona's back was turned, Miranda was thinking. The poor employee who aspired to the affections of the master, while all the while everyone knew he would marry Shona! What a fool she had made of herself!

Later that night when she was seated before her dressing-table drawing the brush through her hair in preparation for going to bed there was a soft gentle rapping on her door, and when she called 'Come in' she was astonished to find that her visitor was Shona. She was wearing a beautiful cherry-red dressing-gown that draped in rich folds about her small figure, and her soft curls fell in childlike ringlets on her shoulders. She remained at the door and put in her lovely face timidly. 'May I really come in?' she asked softly. 'Or are you terribly, terribly cross with me?'

Miranda stared at her in astonishment. 'No, of course not. Do come in,' she invited.

Shona advanced into the room. 'I simply couldn't go to bed without asking you to forgive me for that horrible, horrible display,' she said pleadingly. 'I can't think what came over me. But in a way I think it was Auntie's fault. She's the most dreadful person to go shopping with—she wants me to buy things that I really don't care for; she treats me like a child, and sometimes it can be dreadfully annoying. I expect I was tired. It's not like me to say all those horrid things. You do forgive me, don't you?'

'Of course,' Miranda agreed instantly. 'You know, Shona, I didn't really want to go the walk with Graham. I mean, I didn't intend to, you see—Well, anyway, I went and——'

'And Graham's so attractive that it's hard to resist him! Don't you find that so?' Shona regarded her with wide gentian-blue eyes.

'Attractive?' Miranda echoed.

Yes, she found Graham attractive—too much so, Miranda was thinking. But she had no intention of admitting this to Shona.

'Graham's character is really no concern of mine,' she said stiffly.

'Oh, don't be so stuffy,' Shona exclaimed. 'There's no reason why you shouldn't say it to me. After all, nearly everyone finds Graham irresistible.'

As Miranda did not reply, Shona went on in an altered tone, 'But that's not really what I intended to ask you. You see, Graham's not really interested in these little parties of mine. He's so masculine and out-going that he finds the little details rather stuffy and boring. That's why I'm asking you to help me.'

'To help you—with the party?' Miranda queried, dismayed.

'Yes, it would be wonderful if you'd help with the decorating of the hall. You're so artistic and have such fresh ideas. And I do so want everything to be marvellous. You see, each year we get a write-up in the local paper. I suppose it's silly of me, but I get a kick out of it. That's why each year I try to go one better than the last.'

'Oh no, Shona,' Miranda cried. 'I really think it would be better if I had nothing to do with it. This is

115

your affair and I'd rather take no part in it.'

'Don't say that!' Shona protested. 'How can you be so cruel?'

'But I ought to stick to what I'm paid for,' Miranda told her. 'You must see that, Shona.'

'But this party is for *me*,' Shona assured her. 'If you think Graham might object you can just forget it. He would be only delighted if you would do anything to help me.'

'No, Shona,' Miranda said, 'It simply wouldn't do at all. I don't want to step out of line again.'

'So you haven't forgiven me, is that it?' Shona cried, disappointed. 'You would help me, only you're still annoyed with me because I said all those horrid things. And I'm so truly sorry for them too.'

'It's not that, Shona,' Miranda began.

But tears had flooded into Shona's beautiful eyes. 'Yes, it is,' she said brokenly. 'I can see you'll never, never forgive me. Oh, why, why did I say those things—especially when I didn't for a moment mean them.'

'But I do forgive you! Really I do,' Miranda assured her.

'Then you will come and help me.' Immediately Shona had brightened. 'I knew you wouldn't be so horrid as to keep up a grudge. Not when you're so generous and such a fine person! I do admire you, Miranda, because you're so clever and have such personality, and—— You'll promise to help won't you—otherwise I'll know that what I said was unforgivable.'

'All right then! If that's the way you're going to take it,' Miranda yielded with a sigh.

'Oh, you are a darling!' Shona cried, all smiles. She

rushed towards Miranda, gave her a swift hug and then scuttled from the room, her small feet pattering across the floor in fluffy mules.

When she had gone Miranda slowly turned back to her mirror, and resumed brushing her hair. The quarrel with Shona was made up, she was thinking, and that was a good thing, because she didn't want to be at enmity with her. But she felt doubtful about this promise to help decorate the hall for the party. Shona had assured her that Graham would be delighted, but would he be? Would he perhaps regard it as an interference on her part, an attempt to push herself forward and to take out of Shona's hands the work in which she delighted? This could easily give him the wrong impression and Esther Gregg would make no attempt to protect her should he regard her presence as an intrusion. As for Shona, she was so deeply in love with Graham that his approval was all that mattered to her.

In agreeing to have any part in this affair she had blundered once again, Miranda felt. It would turn out badly, of that she was convinced.

When the day arrived when they were to decorate the hall Miranda felt her spirits sink. Normally it was a task she would have delighted in, but she was no longer at ease with Shona. Good-humoured as the girl had appeared, Miranda had the uncomfortable feeling that in her company she should step warily. An incautious, or tactless remark could easily bring about one of those tearful and upsetting scenes, which somehow always left Miranda feeling horribly in the wrong.

As her Aunt Esther had remarked, Shona was

extraordinarily sensitive, which made friendship with her a hazardous business.

Before going downstairs Miranda slipped into well-worn jeans and tied her hair back with a tartan ribbon.

When she arrived in the long Jacobean hall where the party was to be held she found an enormous fire crackling cheerfully in the huge stone chimneyplace, and Shona standing a little disconsolately, a bundle of coloured balloons in her hand, at the foot of a step-ladder.

'Oh, there you are!' she exclaimed, brightening as she saw Miranda appear. 'I'm so glad you're here. I thought for a minute you might have backed out—but then I know you're not that sort of person! Have you any idea how we should arrange the balloons? I thought of hanging them from the rafters, but I've no head for heights, and anyway it would take ages to fix them all.' She pointed to boxes piled on the long refectory table. 'I must say the idea of blowing them all up and tying them on makes me quail. Besides, as I said, heights give me vertigo.'

Miranda considered. 'What about arranging the frieze about the walls and having bunches of different coloured balloons in each corner? We could have masses and masses of them, and they'd look very effective.'

Shona nodded. 'Yes, that's a splendid idea! And besides, it would be so much quicker.'

She paused and glanced at her watch, then gave a little exclamation of dismay. 'Would you be an angel and fix it for me, Miranda? I've got to go up to Glasgow to collect my dress. You see, I always wear a very special outfit for these parties, something very gay and colourful for the children's sake. They love that sort of thing. I think on the whole grown-ups have the idea children don't notice, but they do, you know. That's why I always make a special effort to look nice and festive for the occasion.'

'You mean, you want me to do all the decoration?' Miranda asked a little helplessly, glancing at the step-ladder and the boxes piled with paper hats, crackers, and false faces.

Shona looked at her appealingly. 'I should be so grateful if you would. Besides, you've all sorts of wonderful and original ideas. You'd be so much better at the job than I should.'

In spite of the fact that she realised that Shona was flattering her, Miranda found it hard to resist the appealing look in the wide eyes.

'Well, I'll try,' Miranda said reluctantly. 'But suppose you don't like my efforts when you come back.'

Shona looked hurt at the suggestion. 'But of course I'll like anything you do! You're so frightfully artistic. You mustn't think me a horrid ungrateful beast and imagine I'd be critical and carping.'

As she listened Miranda found herself feeling in the wrong—but Shona frequently made her feel that way.

Then, looking very satisfied with herself, Shona hurried away.

Standing alone in the huge hall, Miranda began to visualise how she would hang the decorations.

First, she decided, she would lay the frieze against the walls. It would certainly look dramatic running above the panelling, the silver witch riding her broom against a huge golden moon that rode in a midnight-blue sky. She would make great clusters of multi-coloured balloons and place them like bunches of hanging grapes in each corner.

She visualised how the long table would look, covered with all the goodies children love, and piled with dishes of nuts, fruit and crackers. Along the centre would be spaced the pumpkins in crimson, green, yellow and red, and glowing with hidden lights.

She began work and was on the top of the steps fixing the frieze to the panelling with drawing-pins when Graham appeared in the doorway.

He glanced about, then, hands in pockets, casually strolled towards the ladder. 'I don't see Shona about,' he remarked.

Miranda gazed down from her perch. 'No. She had to go to Glasgow to fetch her dress for the party.'

'Collect a dress? Well, this is the first I've heard of it.'

'Perhaps she wanted to surprise you!' Miranda smiled.

He grimaced wryly. 'The trouble with Shona is she goes in for too many surprises. Anyway, she has lots of clothes. I should have imagined she'd have been able to discover something in her wardrobe suitable for the occasion.'

'That shows how little you know of women,' Miranda told him.

'You're probably right! But it amazes me that you're taking her desertion so coolly, considering you've been left to do all the donkey-work,' he remarked.

'Oh but I enjoy it,' she told him, reaching higher to fix a drawing pin that had slipped from its place.

'You don't mean to say you blew up all those balloons yourself?' he asked incredulously, eyeing a great bunch which she had attached to a nail in readiness to be hung.

120

'Yes, and I've lots more to do yet,' Miranda told him as she caught the great cluster of balloons and reached out to fasten it to a nail high in the corner of the room.

'Then it looks to me as if it's time I lent a hand,' he said briskly, 'because it looks to me that if you take on any more you'll float through the window. You're far too slight and ethereal-looking for that job.'

'Oh, but I'm not,' Miranda assured him laughingly. 'I'm extremely tough. You'd be surprised at some of my feats of strength.'

'But the nail's way out of your reach! I suggest you let me take over, and you can direct operations from below.'

Miranda looked down at him doubtfully. 'Oh, but I've a plan in my mind of exactly how I want the hall to look. You'd probably put the decorations up any old how.'

'My dear girl, you can trust me implicitly,' he assured her solemnly. 'A Lairdlaw's word is his bond. If you place your balloons in my keeping, I shall cherish them with my life.'

'Well—as long as you follow my instructions,' Miranda told him severely, trying to hold back a laugh.

And with a sigh of relief she began to climb down the ladder, only then realizing how stiff her arms had become from stretching them while pinning on the frieze.

'We'll do the rest of the balloons first,' she said, 'then tie them into bunches.'

Together they crossed to the table and energetically began blowing up the balloons, occasionally dissolving into hilarious laughter, when they caught a glimpse of their distended cheeks in a wall mirror.

Then very deliberately Graham blew up a multi-coloured balloon until it became huge, and Miranda closed her eyes and placed her fingers in her ears as she waited for the inevitable explosion. When it came, it was much louder than she had expected. Involuntarily she jerked her head, and the tartan ribbon which tied her ponytail, and which had gradually been slipping further and further down on her silky hair, fell to the floor.

She bent to retrieve it, but Graham was before her and snatching it up held it above his head, well out of her reach.

'Before I give it back to you, you must answer a question,' he explained. 'Otherwise you forfeit the ribbon.'

'It depends what the question is,' Miranda replied cautiously.

'Well, here goes! You must tell me why you're wearing a tartan ribbon. Can it be because you're becoming Scottish at heart? I'll give you five seconds in which to answer, and if I don't get a satisfactory reply, I shall confiscate it.'

Half laughing, half exasperated, Miranda made futile little jumps and tried in vain to snatch it back, but he was much too quick for her, and she was on the point of giving up and composing some sort of evasive answer when she realised that Mrs Gilmore had appeared.

'I thought I heard a bang as I was passing,' she remarked. But Miranda could see from her expression that she must have witnessed some of her wild leaps in an effort to retrieve her property; she felt hot with embarrassment, and turned her head away. What must the prim and proper Mrs Gilmore think of her extraordinary antics!

'I was wondering if you'd like a cup of coffee,' Mrs Gilmore went on, in an obvious effort to smooth over the embarrassing moment.

'An excellent idea, Mrs Gilmore,' Graham agreed, evidently completely unmoved by the fact that she had witnessed the incident.

As he spoke he slipped the tartan ribbon into his pocket, and Miranda, seeing this, was struck by the thought that possibly he was secretly as uncomfortable as she was that Mrs Gilmore had seen his unlairdlike behaviour. Later on, when they were alone once more, Graham would, no doubt, return it to her

He pulled up huge comfortable armchairs to the roaring fire and together they sat there sipping the delicious coffee and nibbling the shortbread biscuits Mrs Gilmore had provided.

He looked across at her his eyes intent and asked suddenly, 'Are you happy here, Miranda?'

She glanced down at her steaming cup in an effort to evade his gaze. 'But of course! I love the work. After all, it's what I've been trained to do. I consider myself very lucky to have this job.'

'And it will lead to better things! Isn't that what you expect?' he asked dryly.

She stared into the flames thoughtfully. 'I don't really think of it that way.'

'No? I don't suppose you do. It was rather unfair of me to ask that.'

He bent down absently and picked up a blue and gold cracker which had rolled from the table and fallen to the floor; he turned it between his strong, well-shaped fingers, and smiled a little wryly as he examined it.

'When I was a child the crackers were the best part of any party—apart from the satisfying bang there was the motto and the gift. What do you say we pull this one now and see what the gods will send us?'

He held it out to her and, feeling foolish and elated at the same time, she pulled it with him. The bang was a distinct disappointment, in fact it was hardly audible.

Graham shook his head in disgust. 'Not up to standard, I'm afraid. Let's hope the motto and gift make up for our disappointment!'

But the gift when it was retrieved also proved to be not up to scratch—a small wooden whistle which refused to give the smallest squeak no matter how vigorously Graham blew it.

The motto, however, was a different affair. Miranda picked it up, read it and was on the point of crumpling it and tossing it into the fire when Graham inquired, 'Well, what words of wisdom does it contain? Or is it one of those awful riddles that it would take an Einstein to solve?'

'It's not a riddle,' Miranda told him.

She hoped he would think the pinkness that had risen to her cheeks was due to the warmth of the fire.

'Well, let's hear the worst!' he insisted.

Miranda tried to keep her voice neutral as she read, 'My true love hath my heart, and I have his.'

There was a long silence and when she raised her eyes it was to find Graham looking at her with a strange half-questioning glance that made her heart give a little bound and then beat rather quickly.

'The man who wrote those words obviously believed in them,' said Graham.

Miranda glanced down at the slip of paper, and read solemnly, 'Sir Philip Sidney 1554–1586.'

He nodded. 'This love business has been going on for some time, that's obvious!'

Again an awkward pause followed, and Miranda crumpled up the motto and tossed it into the depths of the flames.

'Mottoes are always so stupid! You'd think they could use something original for a change!'

He glanced across at her, his eyes quizzical. 'Oh, but the motto is an extremely important part of the cracker—if one is in the proper state of mind, that is: it can convey all sorts of information.'

She frowned. 'What do you mean by the proper state of mind, may I ask?'

'Most girls dream that their prince will arrive sooner or later, preferably someone rich or famous, so you can see why the message in the cracker is so important.'

'I can assure you that I don't for one minute imagine that my prince will arrive,' Miranda told him warmly.

'You mean you don't believe in love then?' he exclaimed in mock disbelief. 'What an extraordinary statement from such a pretty girl!'

'I don't mean I don't believe in love,' she put in quickly, 'but I certainly don't believe that the man I fall in love with will be either rich or famous.'

'Ah then, so you believe in love in a cottage? Is that it?'

Miranda was on the point of making a heated reply, when she bit back the words.

The conversation was becoming uncomfortably personal. It would be much better if Graham knew as little as possible about her secret dreams, she told herself, for she suspected that he would be ruthless enough to use such information against her later on, if it suited his purpose.

'I think it's time we got back to work,' she told him firmly, as she replaced her cup and saucer on the tray.

'You're a little slave-driver,' he grumbled, as he reluctantly got to his feet. 'I suspect you're deliberately evading giving me a straight answer.'

'And suppose I am?' she retorted demurely. 'We don't know each other well enough to be exchanging confidences, do we?'

'You'd be surprised how much I know about you already, Miranda Lorimer!'

'Here, take these,' Miranda instructed, pushing into his hands some tiny lanterns. 'I want a row of these strung along the rafters in the centre.'

Graham sighed. 'I guessed, right from the beginning when I found you in the gallery that evening, that I'd taken on a handful.'

Miranda, confident that the moment of danger had passed, followed him half way up the stepladder, bearing a second lantern.

He had placed the first lantern exactly where she wanted it and was leaning down to take from her the second which she was holding up towards him when, without the smallest warning, he pulled her up towards him and kissed her firmly on the lips.

Bewildered by the suddenness of his action, Miranda offered no resistance—and it was at this moment that Shona chose to return.

Over Graham's shoulder Miranda saw her standing in the doorway, clutching an enormous box. Under her fluffy fur hat, her face was white and shocked.

Was it a trick of the firelight, Miranda wondered, that the wide kittenish eyes seemed to be narrowed with feline malice and the sweet lips pulled into a hard, thin line?

The little tableau lasted only for a few seconds, but to Miranda it seemed to stretch endlessly. Then Graham released her.

Shona advanced into the room, smiling happily and Miranda wondered if she had only dreamed that momentary transformation.

'How lovely everything looks!' Shona exclaimed. 'You two have been working so hard! Later on, I'll show you my dress, Miranda,' she said. 'But I do insist you have a rest now. You look utterly exhausted.'

In spite of the apparent solicitude of the words, Miranda realised that she was being told in no uncertain manner that her presence was no longer desired.

Quietly she laid down the lantern and walked towards the door. But before she left the hall, she could not resist stealing a covert glance.

She saw Shona walk towards Graham and throw her arms about his shoulders in the naïve, childish, confiding manner that was habitual with her. It would be hard for any man—and especially Graham Lairdlaw—to resist such a woman.

And as she made her way through the chill corridors to her room, Miranda wondered why the knowledge filled her heart with such desolation.

CHAPTER EIGHT

EARLY on the afternoon of the children's party, Miranda found herself bustling between the kitchens and hall, helping Mrs Gilmore and Ida to arrange plates of jellies, custards and cakes, bowls of fruit and nuts and gaily wrapped sweets on the long refectory table. Then the pumpkin lanterns were put in place and surrounded by piles of crimson and gold crackers.

When everything was in order, Miranda stood back to admire the effect. She made a few final touches, and then subsided into one of the wide, wing-backed chairs before the blazing fire, for the luxury of a short respite before the arrival of the children.

Shona had taken no part in these final preparations, remarking that as there were three of them on the job she would only be in the way. She had retired to her room where she was presumably occupied in getting ready to look as pretty as possible for the occasion.

Esther too had retreated; she had gone off to the parlour, saying that she could never abide sticky, excited children and that, anyway, she had a number of letters to write.

So it had happened that it was Miranda who found herself in charge at the end!

'Well, you certainly look tuckered out!' Graham remarked as he came in and surveyed the scene.

She sat up, feeling dishevelled, and hastily smoothed back her hair.

'I'd better tidy up before the party begins,' she told him.

'No, don't try to titivate! You look perfectly charming as you are—in a fey, elfish sort of way.'

'I don't feel at all elfish,' she assured him with a laugh, and wished she had not decided on wearing slacks and T-shirt as being the most practical outfit for the occasion, although the shirt was gaily patterned with flying birds and exotic fruits, she had the feeling that, compared to Shona, she would present a very drab figure indeed.

'Where's Shona?' Graham inquired.

'She's gone upstairs to change.'

'Leaving you to make the last-minute decisions!'

'There was nothing much to be done,' Miranda told him. 'And anyway, I'm ready. I didn't put on anything elaborate, because I know how strenuous these parties can be. Children seem to have an endless fund of energy. By the way, you haven't by any chance decided to lend a hand?'

'Afraid not,' he said hastily. 'I've no talent whatsoever when it comes to organising games of blind man's buff. Anyway, I have only a moment or two to spare. I have to see Andy Blair this afternoon about the chalets. I shall be quite busy enough, I can assure you. In a place like this, there's never an idle moment.'

'Trust a man to wriggle out of things!' Miranda said tartly.

'Do you hate it so much, then?'

'Actually I'm looking forward to it very much—strange as it may seem to you!'

'You mean that as soon as the party begins you'll recover, and be all energy?'

'I always am,' she told him. 'Especially if I'm looking forward to something!'

'In that case, you have a lot in common with Mary Queen of Scots. She once rode fifty miles in a day to see the Earl of Bothwell when he'd been wounded on a foray into England. But then, of course, she was going to see the man she loved. I suppose that made all the difference!'

'Yes, I imagine it would!' Miranda replied. 'Though he must have been particularly fascinating.'

'According to all accounts the Earl of Bothwell was a real lady-killer, a fairly rough diamond; a Border riever, who made forays into England and was no respecter of courtly manners. Not the type of man, one would think, who would appeal to Mary! But then you never can tell with women, can you?'

Did Graham realise how like he was to the man he had just described? she wondered. She was suddenly aware of how close to her chair he was standing, and bending forward she began furiously to poke the fire.

'I expect she found him attractive because it would be such a change from being constantly fawned on by obsequious courtiers,' she said.

'So you too prefer the Border bandit type? Is that it?'

'I didn't say that!' she told him hastily.

'All right, then! Lay your cards on the table! What kind of man would you fall for?'

'It's—it's hard to tell,' she replied evasively. 'When a girl is young she's attracted to a completely different type of man from the kind she cares for as she grows older.'

'You're deliberately avoiding the issue,' he accused. 'Why can't you state here and now the kind of man you're likely to fall for? And if you prefer the hot-blooded riever type don't hesitate to state it plainly. *I* certainly shan't mind. After all, I'm the complete opposite—a rather placid, humdrum, introvert type, anxious to please, and——'

'You're not a bit like that!' Miranda contradicted hotly. 'Why, you're the most arrogant and despotic, self-opinionated man—'

Graham held up his hand. 'Enough, enough! I get the general idea. In other words, you dislike me intensely.'

Miranda's eyes widened. 'Oh no, I didn't say that,' she protested.

'Indeed! Do you, by any chance, imagine you were being complimentary?'

'Well, you can be pretty horrid, when you want to,' she informed him.

'True! Perhaps at moments I may be rather irascible,' he conceded. 'But, with you, I have the feeling I could not be at cross purposes for long.'

His voice was low and held a note of significance that gave Miranda a moment of sudden, unaccountable happiness.

He stretched out his hand and gently disentangled a wisp of glittering tinsel from her hair. His fingers seemed to hold a caress and Miranda felt her heart beat uncomfortably fast.

In an effort to appear composed, she said accusingly, 'By the way, you don't happen to have the ribbon I lost when we were hanging the decorations?'

'Ribbon?' he echoed.

'Yes, and I'd like it back, please. It was a particular favourite of mine.'

'I'm afraid I haven't the slightest idea what you're talking about,' he replied. 'However, if I do happen to see it knocking about, you may be sure I'll return it immediately.'

'Oh, you're impossible!' Miranda exclaimed, getting to her feet. 'You know perfectly well that you——' She stopped. To admit that she had seen him put it in his pocket would somehow spoil this tenuous thread of understanding that seemed to lie between them.

'All right! All right!' he said. 'I know when I'm not wanted!' He turned and laughingly retreated from the hall.

And Miranda, watching him go, wished suddenly that she could keep him by her side. But it was a dangerous thought, she knew, and she determined to shrug it off.

It was then she became aware that she was being watched by Esther. The older woman stood at the foot of the stairs gazing into the long hall through the open lancet door.

How long had she been there? Miranda wondered. Had she seen Graham gently touch her hair and had she perhaps misinterpreted the gesture. She felt uncomfortable and faintly guilty as Esther walked towards her. But Esther made no reference to the incident as she handed Miranda a bundle of letters. 'I want someone to go down to the post with these right away,' she told her. 'And as you don't seem to be doing anything at the moment I'd be grateful if you'd go. But do hurry! You'll just manage to catch it, if you put a spurt on.'

It was on the tip of Miranda's tongue to tell Esther that she had no intention whatsoever of acting as her messenger, but she decided, on second thoughts, that she would undertake the commission. There was no sense in quarrelling with the older woman and it would sound churlish to give a blank refusal.

'Very well,' she said, none too graciously, but as she

took the letters from Esther she was thinking that a walk in the crisp autumn air would refresh her and blow away the cobwebs for the hectic hours that lay ahead.

But as she hurried towards the village she was feeling rather resentful: it was not that she objected to doing small favours—especially when it was the case of an older woman. But she found Mrs Gregg's high-handed manner particularly annoying, especially as Shona was always treated as a piece of the most delicate porcelain. The way Esther differentiated between them was mortifying and wounding.

As she approached the village she caught a glimpse of the postman emptying the box in the centre of the cluster of houses that formed the hamlet of Drumdarrow: she broke into a run and was just in time for him to take the letters from her and to thrust them into his bag with an amused smile.

As she turned back she found herself face to face with Andy Blair.

'Have you ambitions to compete in the Olympics?' he asked. 'That was quite a sprint—I was filled with admiration.'

So he had witnessed her undignified dash towards the pillarbox, she thought a little uncomfortably.

'They must have been very important when you were in such a hurry about them.'

'Oh, they're not mine,' she told him, instantly regretting her words, as he said,

'So you were on an errand for His Royal Highness, Graham Lairdlaw! No doubt you were instructed not, on peril of your life, to miss the afternoon post. He seems to have forgotten that you were engaged to take care of the collection—not to act as messenger.'

'Oh, but they're not Graham's,' she told him.

'Shona's, then?'

'No, not Shona's either,' Miranda returned with a smile.

There was something almost childish about Andy's open curiosity and dislike of the household at the Castle. And somehow his attitude seemed to have restored her to good humour.

He smiled, and Miranda was reminded of Shona's remark that Andy Blair was handsome. His delicate, regular features showed to advantage when his face was free from his habitual sullen look of resentment and self-pity.

'Tell me, must you hurry back, or have you time for a coffee?' he asked suddenly.

Miranda hesitated. 'I suppose I should be getting back, but everything's in pretty good order, so I don't see why I shouldn't take a small break.'

'Good,' he said, taking her arm and leading her along the pavement.

'But I've promised to help with the children's party,' she warned, 'so I haven't much time.'

'Don't worry. You'll be back in good time: I'll see to that,' he told her. 'Jessie McAlpine "does" teas for the summer visitors and I think I might be able to persuade her to rustle up a cup of coffee for us quickly.'

He stopped outside the door of a small house built of softly coloured stone that seemed to blend with the strange pastel, fairy-tale colours of the district.

Here, at a little table spread with a tartan cloth in reds and greens, they had coffee in one of the small front rooms. And Miranda found that Andy, when he exerted himself, could be extremely pleasant company.

134

There was only one moment that she found slightly surprising and faintly puzzling. As Jessie, a squat, red-faced woman, placed upon the table a steaming pot of coffee, with cream and home-made scones, she fixed Andy with a knowing regard.

'So Cynthia Rawlinson has gone home, has she?' she asked pointedly.

'Yes. In fact, the whole Rawlinson family have gone,' Andy replied smoothly.

'Ah, but it's her you'll miss most of all,' Jessie remarked with a cackle, flicking a crumb from the table with the edge of a snowy napkin.

'That will do, Jessie,' Andy said sharply. 'Get back to your stockpot, like a good woman!'

Somewhat to Miranda's surprise, Jessie, instead of showing resentment at his curt dismissal, gave a crow of laughter and marched out of the room with a grin on her broad face.

When she had gone, Andy said smoothly, 'You didn't meet the Rawlinsons while they were here, did you? They took one of the chalets for a fortnight's late holiday and made it a centre for touring the district. Cynthia was fun, but unfortunately became rather a bore towards the end: so many women want to make something permanent out of what can never be more than a holiday romance! It's rather a pity really, because they spoil things!'

Miranda was silent. This was a side of Andy's character that was news to her. But after all, she told herself, Andy Blair's love life was none of her business. And, even if he didn't appear to be a particularly nice person, he was an amusing and diverting companion for the time being.

'By the way, you haven't changed your mind about

taking a chalet, have you?' Andy inquired.

Miranda looked at him in surprise. 'No, why should I?'

'It struck me that the atmosphere at Drumdarrow might not be too congenial. Esther Gregg is rather a witch—not to speak of Shona! Now there's a girl who would make a very dangerous adversary indeed! Take my advice and watch your step where she's concerned, Miranda.'

Miranda laid down her cup and regarded him with astonishment. 'I don't know how you can say such a thing. Shona has shown me nothing but friendship since she came.'

'All the same, I'd be careful, if I were you. I know her a great deal better than you do, remember! You should be very wary as far as that girl is concerned,' he reiterated.

For a moment Miranda wondered if she should tell him bluntly that she resented his criticisms of her friend, then decided not to. After all, Shona was a charming and beautiful girl, and Andy—to say the least of it—was obviously a lady's man. Probably he had tried to flirt too outrageously with her, and had been firmly put in his place. His attack on Shona could easily have been caused by wounded pride.

'If you should find the atmosphere at Drumdarrow getting a bit too fraught, and should change your mind, you'll find me at the first chalet. You can't miss it: it's the only black-and-white one. The chalet I showed you is still vacant; if you want it, I'd make things as cosy as possible. In the meantime, if anyone makes inquiries about it, I'll stall a bit.'

'Don't bother,' Miranda told him, half amused and a little flattered at his insistence. 'I haven't the slightest intention of leaving Drumdarrow. The Castle's a wonderful old place and I love being there. The children's party this afternoon, for instance, I'm going to give a hand with things and I'm quite looking forward to it.'

'Oh yes, Shona's famous Hallowe'en party! So she's roped you in to help! She enjoys playing hostess to the local kids, as long as it doesn't involve her in any work. I suppose it will be the usual do—blind man's buff, ducking for apples, ghost stories, etcetera. I suspect you're in for a pretty hectic time.'

'There are to be no ghost stories,' she told him. 'Not this year! The children, it seems, can be excitable enough, without giving them the horrors into the bargain.'

'But what are you going to do to inject a little novelty into the affair? Perhaps Esther Gregg might oblige by doing conjuring tricks, between telling funny stories.'

The malice was evident in his voice, nevertheless the idea of Esther solemnly pulling rabbits from a hat made Miranda giggle, and Andy, seeing that he had succeeded in amusing her, went from one flight of extravagant fancy to another.

His wit, she noticed, was always turned against someone else. Nevertheless it was clever in its own way, and Miranda, tired after her exertions of the early afternoon, found it entertaining and relaxing.

As they left Jessie's tea-shop they stood on the pavement, laughing and talking together before parting, and it was with something of a shock that Miranda realised that the car parked a little further along the road was Graham's and that the figure getting out of it was Graham himself.

As they drew near he fixed them with a level stare

137

which Miranda found particularly unnerving, and which Andy also seemed to find disconcerting.

'Hello, what are you two doing here? Surely the party is in full swing by now?'

Miranda, with the guilty knowledge that she had lingered far too long over coffee with Andy, said defensively, 'Mrs Gregg sent me to the post with letters.'

'But that must have been some time ago! It must be at least an hour since the post was collected,' he said dryly. 'You'd better get in, and I'll drive you back.'

Then Andy came under his dark regard. 'I was looking for you at the chalets. I've some things to discuss. However, no doubt you found Miranda better company than a dreary business discussion, so it can wait till later.'

With an angry, muttered remark Andy, a sulky and resentful expression once more on his face, turned away and walked off rapidly.

Miranda looked after his departing figure, feeling resentment burning up in her. How dared Graham burst so arrogantly into their company!

She got into the car in angry silence and sat tightly against the door in an effort to dissociate herself.

'You needn't bother yourself sitting there scowling,' he told her, as he swept the car in an arc and set off for the castle, 'because I'm totally indifferent to your moods, my girl!'

So you're indifferent to my moods—but Shona's happiness is everything to you! Miranda was thinking bitterly.

'You seemed to be enjoying a huge joke as you came out of Jessie McAlpine's. I suppose you were having tea and crumpets, and he was being hilarious at someone else's expense!'

'I don't see why you should object to the fact that he's amusing,' Miranda said stiffly. 'Anyway, I like him,' she added defiantly.

'Why? Because he's so handsome? So you accede to the consensus of opinion on that point?'

'I'm not particularly interested in his appearance,' Miranda returned hotly. 'What interests me is his manner. He's so pleasant and civilised and——'

'And such a difference from some boors you could mention! But then perhaps Andy gets more practise than the rest of us! He's rather a lady's man and believes in keeping his hand in with any attractive female he comes across.'

Miranda, remembering Jessie's jollying remarks about Cynthia Rawlinson, remained silent for a moment, then she said, 'Mr Blair's attitude towards women is hardly any of my concern. And anyway, now that you've brought it up, I *do* think he's handsome.'

'In that case it's a pity I broke up your jolly little get-together. I've half a mind to put you out: perhaps if you hurried, you could make up on him.'

'But you won't,' Miranda told him dryly.

'Why not?'

'Because——' But she stopped herself.

She had been about to say, because you want me to be there to assist with the party and to make a success of it—for Shona's sake. The only person you care about is Shona, she wanted to scream at him. Instead, she sat with tight lips and stared fixedly ahead until they reached Drumdarrow.

When they arrived she was immediately plunged into a maelstrom of furious activity and for the following two hours the hall rang and re-echoed with the screams of excited children, and the popping of balloons.

When, at last, the final cracker had been pulled, and the children had reluctantly departed, Shona flung herself back in a chair.

'Well, thank heavens that's over for another year! It's certainly been a strenuous afternoon. I'm completely worn out—although I do think I made a success of it,' she added complacently. 'The children certainly seemed to enjoy themselves, although they've left a hideous mess.' She made a moue of disgust as she stared around.

Miranda had to agree. The once attractively laid refectory table was a scene of desolation, with half-finished plates of custard and jelly, squashed cream cakes, discarded paper hats and cracker wrappers jumbled with battered paper cups and broken straws. The parquet floor had not escaped either: nutshells were scattered on its shining surface and to one side, near the giant gaily painted tub in which the children had ducked for apples, there were signs of water having been hastily mopped up.

This had been the part of the entertainment the children had liked best, wildly plumping their faces into the depths with shrieks of merriment.

Shona stretched lazily. 'I suppose I ought to tidy up. I feel as if I'd been through a force ten gale!'

But Miranda, looking at the immaculate and unruffled Shona, was thinking that it was she herself who needed repairs. She had caught sight of herself in a wall mirror and knew that her hair was thoroughly untidy and that the gaily patterned T-shirt was badly crumpled.

But she felt too lazy and relaxed to go upstairs and tidy up. Instead, she reclined her head against the headrest of her winged chair, closed her eyes and drew a sigh of relief.

It was true, as Shona had remarked, that the party had been an uproarious success as far as the children were concerned. But, in spite of her satisfaction at the thought, she felt a slight twinge of resentment that Shona was adopting the attitude that she had coped with the various crises that had blown up during the previous few hours.

For it had not been Shona who had mopped up when custard had been spilt on the floor: it was not Shona who had soothed screaming, over-excited children after games of blind man's buff and hide-and-seek: it was not Shona who had patiently played the piano for musical chairs. In fact, it had not been Shona who had organised the games: not Shona who had separated bellicose little boys who, for no apparent reason, had sprung at each other in bouts of furious fisticuffs.

It seemed unfair that Shona should claim the credit of the success of the party, when, in fact, her main occupation had been to float about looking beautiful in her lovely new dress.

It certainly was exquisite, Miranda was thinking: composed of layers of finest silk voile, shading from palest lime green to jade and deep glowing peacock: a dress in which the different layers of the diaphanous material seemed to be a shifting amalgam of gently shaded greens. It had been clear that the little girls especially had been entranced by its beauty as she moved among them like an ethereal princess in a fairy-tale.

When Graham came in, Shona sprang to her feet and ran across the hall to slip her arm through his.

'Now that the children are safely home again, let's have a little fun ourselves,' she coaxed.

'Like what?' he asked, as he subsided into a chair.

'Let's open a bottle of wine and have a little party,' Shona suggested eagerly.

He smiled at her with that indulgent look that Miranda had come to know so well—and of which she knew herself to be jealous, although she tried hard not to be.

For a moment she deliberately tried to see Shona through his eyes—the soft silver fair curls framing the small, exquisite features, the slim perfect figure in the floating, ever-changing colours of her filmy dress! What a delightful picture she presented, especially when she turned her small face towards him with that expression, so coaxing and so feminine!

'Whatever you say,' he agreed. And very shortly they were sipping sherry and the hall had taken on an air of quiet festivity.

'It's not really Hallowe'en without games,' Shona remarked at last. 'I wish I could think of something really exciting. I'm afraid we're too old for blind man's buff or musical chairs,' she added regretfully.

'Yes, I'm afraid we are—and I can't say I'm altogether sorry,' Graham said dryly.

'Oh, don't be such an old stuffed shirt!' Shona pouted. 'I expect you'd be perfectly happy staring into the fire.'

'Well, actually that's what I enjoy most,' he replied. 'After all, I've had a busy day too.'

'Well, this is not my idea of a festive occasion,' Shona persisted. 'Can you think of something, Mir-

142

anda? Something really exciting!'

Miranda smiled. 'I'm afraid not! When I was a little girl we used to play all the ordinary games—musical chairs, hide-and-seek, hunt the slipper—that sort of thing!'

'Those are old hat,' Shona said impatiently. 'I mean something really interesting.'

'Spare us ghost stories,' Graham begged.

'Oh no, not ghost stories,' Shona agreed. She shuddered, and drew close to Graham. 'They terrify me, although I know most of them are rubbish. All the same, they give me the horrors.'

'There was one special Hallowe'en game,' Miranda recalled. 'But I'm afraid it's not particularly exciting. In fact, it's rather silly.'

'Come on, what was it?' Shona insisted.

'We used to peel an apple and then throw the peel over our shoulder, and——'

Here Miranda stopped, feeling rather silly, and wishing she had not begun the subject.

'Go on. I'm dying to know,' Shona insisted.

'Well, as I told you—it's really a silly idea—but we used to be told that the peel might fall into the initial of the man we would fall in love with.'

'At least it sounds a bit more adult than musical chairs,' Shona said. 'You must peel an apple and demonstrate, Miranda.' With almost childish eagerness, she ran towards the table, picked up a knife and selecting a large rosy apple from a bowl presented them to Miranda. 'Now you must demonstrate,' she commanded.

Feeling rather foolish, Miranda began to peel it thinly, taking care to make it continuous. When she had a long thin strand of peel, she gathered it together carefully, stood up and threw it over her shoulder, very conscious of Shona's eager absorption and her sudden silence as it fell to the floor.

'Well,' she laughed, 'tell me the worst!'

But as there was still no sound from Shona she turned to look. Her eyes widened, for the thin crimson strand of peel had distinctly formed the shape of the letter G.

The silence was now almost palpable.

'I did tell you it was a silly sort of game,' Miranda said, conscious that her voice sounded high and artificial.

But Shona didn't appear to hear her.

'It *is* a G, isn't it?' she challenged.

'It—it might be,' Miranda found herself saying weakly. There was something distinctly unnerving in Shona's wide regard.

'Nonsense, there's no "might" about it,' Shona said sharply. 'It's very definitely a G.'

'Miranda's right,' Graham interposed, a thin edge of irritation in his voice. 'This is rather a silly game, and I suggest we give it a miss.'

'Oh no, Graham,' Shona said quite sharply. 'Not before Miranda answers some questions. I want to know, Miranda, if you ever knew a man whose christian name began with G.'

'But, Shona, it's only a game,' Miranda found herself muttering uneasily.

Shona stamped her foot in childish impatience. 'No, I insist! Did you, or did you not, have a boy-friend whose name began with G?'

Miranda glanced in Graham's direction, but she was not to find any support in that quarter, for Graham merely looked at her with an expression that

144

held more than a hint of derision. His attitude strengthened her decision not to allow herself to be browbeaten.

'As a matter of fact, no, I didn't,' she told Shona coolly.

She saw the girl bite her lower lip, as though in an effort to control an angry outburst.

Shona gave a high, brittle laugh. 'Well, it certainly couldn't be G for Graham! That would be too ridiculous, wouldn't it?'

'This has gone on long enough,' Graham interposed. He stooped, and picking up the peel tossed it decisively into the fire. 'We've had enough of this silliness: let's change the subject, shall we? Tell me, how did the party go?'

'Oh, wonderfully,' Shona replied without enthusiasm. 'The children simply loved it.'

'Well, it's a comfort to know they haven't been quite as messy as they usually are,' Graham remarked. 'Last year the floor was awash when they'd ducked for apples. And as to custard and jellies and other assorted edibles, they seemed to have thrown more around than they'd eaten!'

'They were just as bad this year,' Shona admitted. 'But then children can't enjoy themselves if they have to be watchful all the time. The worst was mopped up before you made your appearance. Which all goes to show what a dragon you are, Graham!'

'I see. And who effected the transformation?' Graham asked idly.

'Miranda did. She was simply wonderful. She mopped up the water and wiped all the sticky faces and hands. Then there was that dear little fair-haired boy who spilt all the lemonade. She really was a perfect

145

angel,' Shona told him in her high, childish voice.

Miranda breathed a sigh of relief. Shona had apparently forgotten the wretched incident with the apple peel. She had feared for a moment that a storm was about to blow up, but now it seemed that all was happily forgotten.

Eagerly she attempted to meet the girl half way.

'It was no trouble,' she said warmly. 'Anyway, I was dressed for the job! It was much more sensible to leave it to me! It would have been a terrible pity to have ruined your lovely dress cleaning up after the children.'

To her dismay, she saw Shona's face stiffen with affront, and tears gather in her wide eyes.

'How could you say such a horrid thing?' she whispered in a broken voice. 'To insinuate that I left all the nasty jobs to you, just because I was thinking of my dress all the time! It makes me sound so lazy and selfish and——'

She crossed to Graham and laid her head on his shoulder, as though seeking comfort, tears spilling down her faintly flushed cheeks.

Graham's arm drew her close. He laid his cheek against her soft white-blonde curls, and over her head regarded Miranda with a cold, accusing stare.

'But then Miranda's so efficient! With Miranda on the job, nothing can go wrong!' he said sardonically. 'She's rather like Andy Blair in that respect. He's a most efficient person too! I should imagine they'd get on very well together.'

Miranda rose slowly to her feet, feeling the blood drain from her face. What had she done to deserve such a scathing attack? Surely Graham didn't really believe that her remarks had been intended as snide digs at Shona. She felt her throat tighten and, for a horrible moment, felt that she too was going to burst into tears. But pride came to her rescue and, turning, she walked swiftly from the room.

In her bedroom she marched up and down struggling with a feeling that was an amalgam of misery and fury. To think that she had worked so hard to make the party a succes, only to have it result in such a painful and humiliating débâcle! But then she had suspected, right from the start, that she shouldn't involve herself in the party.

Could Shona's extraordinary outburst have been caused by the ridiculous game with the apple peel? Surely the girl didn't truly believe that the remarks about her dress had contained a covert criticism of her behaviour!

Miranda pushed her hair back from her forehead: anger and excitement, and the disturbing suspicion that Shona was not as naïve as she appeared, made her thoughts whirl.

Suddenly she stopped in her march back and forth across the big room. Esther Gregg had been right in advising her to leave the Castle, she thought bitterly. She would not stay another night under Graham Lairdlaw's roof, she determined. But on the other hand, pride would not allow her to give up her job and to skulk away like a criminal. No, she would continue her work at the Castle, but in future she would be very careful not to allow herself to become involved in any way with its inhabitants.

She would have no difficulty in finding accommodation, she knew. Andy Blair would have a tenant for the vacant chalet much sooner than he expected, she thought grimly.

She dragged a suitcase out of one of the big cupboards and began to pack. She would take only enough for the night, she decided. On the following day she would make a clean sweep of her possessions. It would be wonderful to be independent, to have a place of her own, she told herself without conviction.

Unhappiness seemed to creep insidiously into her heart like an enveloping fog. There was, too, a niggling little worry at the back of her mind.

Andy Blair, it was clear, considered himself rather a lady-killer. What would be his reaction to her sudden capitulation? And she wondered uneasily just how much of a problem he might prove to be.

CHAPTER NINE

As she opened the tiny wicket gate that led to Andy Blair's chalet, Miranda saw a glimmer of light in the windows. She walked slowly along the short crazy-paved path, and as she did so the feverish sense of urgency that had swept her along seemed to evaporate, now that she was on the point of burning her boats.

She hesitated outside the door.

Were she to turn back now and retrace her steps to the castle she would be able to slip into her room again before anyone had noticed her absence.

She was on the point of turning away when the door was flung open, and Andy stood outlined against the bright, vivid interior. He peered into the dusk, then gave a low whistle as he saw her.

'Don't tell me this is a social visit—it would be too

good to be true.'

'I've—I've come about the vacant chalet,' Miranda blurted.

'So you've changed your mind, after all! Good! Frankly I hadn't much hope that you'd take up my offer so soon! But wonders never cease! But come in and have a drink. You look like Little Orphan Annie, standing out there.'

'No, thanks,' Miranda replied hastily. 'If you give me the key, I'll go along to the chalet and settle in.'

'I'll do better than that! I'll take you along myself and see you're fixed in nice and cosy.'

'No, no!' Miranda expostulated. 'I can manage. I'd really prefer to go myself.'

'Nonsense! You're only saying that! What girl doesn't want a solicitous cavalier dancing attendance on her!' he chuckled complacently.

In a few moments he reappeared on the doorstep, a bunch of keys in his hand and, taking her suitcase, led her possessively along the path.

'Somehow it's been in the back of my mind that sooner or later you'd turn up. Although I must admit I didn't dream that tonight was going to be my lucky night.'

'What do you mean?' Miranda asked sharply, stopping suddenly in her tracks.

'My, but you are suspicious!' he chuckled. 'All I mean is that it's great to have a pretty girl as a neighbour. At the moment our clientele at the chalets are climbers, or fishermen, or nature-lovers—no sight to gladden a man's eyes, I can tell you! But why the sudden change of heart? You haven't, by any chance, quarrelled with Graham Lairdlaw at last? I always knew it would happen. He's an extremely difficult

149

man to pull with.' His voice had lost its bantering tone: he sounded sour and resentful.

'I don't see why you should assume I have quarrelled with him,' Miranda remarked. 'I've simply decided it would be better to have a place of my own.'

'I see! So snatching up an overnight bag, you rush off at this hour of an autumn evening!'

'It's not so late,' she protested.

'Perhaps not, but it's rather cold and dark. If you haven't quarrelled with him, why did you not wait until tomorrow when you could have settled in in daylight?'

'Because I wanted to leave tonight—and that's that!' she retorted tartly, a little irritated at his persistence.

When they reached the chalet Andy unlocked the door, switched on the light and motioned her in with a flourish. 'You can get settled in while I rustle up some groceries,' he told her. 'But don't worry, I shan't be long. It seems to me that you're badly in need of company.'

When he had gone, Miranda stood looking about despondently. The little house was perfect in every detail, but in miniature, like a doll's house. How pretty and attractive it was! And how she would have revelled in this tiny kingdom at any other time! Here she could work and relax as she wished, yet somehow she felt no sense of anticipation.

She shivered. In spite of its prettiness, it was chilly in the little sitting-room: she switched on the electric fire, crouched down on the thick, silky rug, and held out her hands to the welcome glow.

She must try to make order out of her chaotic thoughts. For one thing, she needn't worry about whether she could afford the rent of this luxury chalet, for Graham had been very generous concerning her salary; she would be able to make this her home until the work was finished; lack of finances would not compel her ignominiously to return to the Castle. Yet the thought afforded her no satisfaction. Instead of feeling warmly secure, she had a sense of being lonely and abandoned, an outcast from the magical world of Drumdarrow—the place in which her heart and all her interests now centred.

But there could be no turning back, she knew. She had definitely burnt her boats. On the following day, thanks to Andy, the whole village would have the news that she had left the Castle.

Andy came in, bearing in his arms a box of groceries.

'I'll dump these in the kitchen,' he told her. 'I simply picked anything that came to hand from my stores; I do hope you find something you like. Anyway, I'll be quite satisfied with whatever menu you decide on. I've a feeling a hot meal would do us both good and probably put you in a more amiable state of mind.'

'What do you mean?' Miranda got to her feet slowly and stared at him. There was something disturbingly aggressive about his manner. 'I—I don't know that I feel much like dinner this evening,' she told him.

'Oh, but I do,' he replied. 'Still, I'm not fussy, and after all, I'm not asking much. I supply the groceries and you dish up the hash—not a bad bargain, I think you'll agree. It will save me making something for myself—a job I heartily detest anyway.'

Feeling too weary and emotionally drained to put

up any serious opposition, Miranda said ungraciously, 'Oh, very well, if you insist!'

'Yes, I do insist,' he replied. 'I'm not the type easily to be squashed, as I suppose you've noticed.'

With as good grace as she could muster, she went into the kitchen and began to unpack the box. Andy followed and stood leaning against the table, hands in pockets, a complacent smile touching the corners of his lips.

'I'm afraid I'm not much of a cook,' she told him ruefully. 'It's something I never seemed to have time to learn properly.'

'What! Do you mean you don't even know how to make scrambled eggs?' he inquired incredulously.

'Well—yes, I could manage that,' Miranda agreed.

'That's marvellous news! You beat up the eggs, while I make the toast,' he instructed.

He produced a shining toaster from a cupboard and, opening a packet of bread, set about the business of toasting in a swift and extremely competent manner.

Miranda could see that he was well used to catering for himself, and wondered why he had been so insistent that she should cook him a meal.

'Isn't this cosy, just the two of us? But then I've always had a hankering for domestic life!' he remarked.

'Then why didn't you get married?' she inquired a little acidly, as she broke some eggs into a basin.

He shrugged. 'I've high standards. The right girl just didn't come along.'

He took a small yellow-and-white checked cloth from a drawer and spread it on the folding table in the dinette.

'I'll not pretend I haven't had lots of girl-friends,' he pursued. 'But I don't intend to plunge into matrimony without giving it due consideration, and I've never met a girl yet who hadn't some vital flaw; either she wasn't pretty enough, or she was too pretty for her own good. Somehow, I've always had the feeling that I'd come across the perfect article some day, and when I did—well, wedding bells for Andy Blair. Who knows, perhaps you're the girl I've been looking for!'

There was something so ludicrously self-satisfied about him that Miranda wondered why she had ever felt the necessity to be wary of him.

'Not bad,' he remarked as she placed a dish of creamy scrambled eggs on the table. 'I expect I could make quite a good cook of you—given time.'

'I don't imagine I'll have much leisure for cookery lessons,' Miranda smiled.

'No. I expect Graham Lairdlaw keeps your nose to the grindstone,' he replied.

'Oh no, it's simply that I like the work,' she told him.

'You mean,' he exclaimed incredulously, 'that you'd rather be up there at the Castle, slogging away, than having a good time?'

'But what exactly do you mean by a good time?'

'Well——' he looked at her knowingly, 'for example, you and I might sample the bright lights some evening when you've finished work. We could drive into Glasgow, see a show, and have a meal afterwards.'

Miranda shook her head. She felt this was the type of invitation she would rather avoid. 'I'm afraid not,' she told him firmly. 'It's not my idea of a good time.'

'Indeed!' he raised his eyebrows. 'Then may I inquire what your idea of a good time is? Most girls would enjoy an evening on the town, especially if they were escorted by a charming and interesting partner.'

His voice was only half bantering and Miranda got the impression that he did in fact imagine that any girl would be flattered to be the object of his attentions.

'What about our making a date?' he persisted.

'No, not just now!' she hedged. 'I'm much too busy.'

'But you must have some spare time! Don't tell me a pretty girl like you is content to stay incarcerated up there at the Castle, immersed in a good book, when you're not working on the collection!'

'I'm perfectly content with my job,' she assured him. She glanced pointedly at her watch. 'It's getting late, and I'm rather tired: I think perhaps it's time you left.'

'Do you, indeed!' Andy's mouth formed into an ugly line. 'So I'm getting the push—is that what you mean? Why the sudden change of mind? I had the strong impression we were all set for an interesting evening together.'

Miranda looked at him blankly. 'Change of mind? What on earth do you mean?'

'Don't give me that stuff! All innocence, aren't you? You know perfectly well what I mean. Am I supposed not to know why you had this sudden yen for the simple life in a chalet? You probably discovered that you don't stand a chance with Graham, now that Shona has appeared on the scene, so you decided that Andy Blair might supply a little diversion. Now, for some reason known only to yourself, you've decided to back out. I think you're going to discover I'm not going to be so easily disposed of.'

His eyes had narrowed viciously and for the first

time Miranda felt a twinge of alarm. She tried to edge towards the door, but found that he had anticipated this move. 'Oh no, you don't! As far as I'm concerned, the evening is just beginning. I'm sure you'll be interested to hear what I have in mind——'

But that was as far as he got.

At that moment the door was thrown open and Graham stood in the entrance regarding the scene in grim silence. Then, without a word, he reached out and catching Miranda roughly by the arm jerked her towards him and marched her swiftly down the path. Still in ominous silence he wrenched open the door of his car, bundled her in, and himself got behind the wheel.

When she had partly recovered from the shock of Graham's appearance, Miranda began to feel a sense of overwhelming resentment at the cavalier way in which he had bundled her out of the chalet and deposited her in the car. She smoothed down her hair, sat bolt upright, and gazed ahead with tight lips. She was being driven towards Drumdarrow, but she was too angry even to put up a protest.

'And now would you mind explaining to me why you left without giving me any warning?' Graham demanded abruptly.

'I don't see that it's any business of yours,' she retorted angrily. 'As long as I'm there to do the work you can have no possible cause for complaint. I'll live where I choose, and you've no right to interfere.'

'It seems to me that I interfered at an opportune moment,' he returned dryly. 'From the look of things, you should be grateful to me for making my appearance when I did.'

'I don't know what you're talking about,' she replied haughtily. 'I was simply having a quiet meal with Andy Blair when you burst in and——'

'Cut it out!' he gritted. 'I know a lot more about Andy Blair than you do. You were a little fool to tear off in that way, without knowing what you were going to get yourself into.'

'If you have such a poor opinion of Andy, why do you keep him on?' she demanded tartly.

'Because he's an extremely good manager! He has his faults, of course, but that's his affair. I didn't expect you to go around hobnobbing with him.'

'I'm not your slave. I'll hobnob with whoever I want to,' she told him furiously.

'Oh no, you won't! Not while you're under my roof!'

'In that case, it would be better if I didn't stay under your roof any longer,' she shot at him.

'Well, you're certainly not going to stay in one of the chalets,' he snapped, 'because I won't allow it.'

'But it's *I* who am paying the rent!' she protested.

'Paying the rent has nothing to do with it! I'm just telling you not to do anything like that again. You're making an utter fool of yourself, only you're too pigheaded to see it. Although I should have guessed you had fallen for him—you made it clear this afternoon.'

For an instant the thought crossed Miranda's mind that it might be her association with Andy that was the cause of Graham's recent irritation with her. But she immediately dismissed this idea as being fantastic. It couldn't possibly matter to Graham whom she made a friend of. No, the simple and obvious explanation was that Graham Lairdlaw was a born autocrat, and didn't intend her to make friends with a man whom he himself disliked.

She tried to sound cool and reasonable. 'Very well then, I'll find lodgings in the village until the work is finished.'

'If you leave Drumdarrow, you won't have a job,' he told her brusquely.

So she was being faced with the alternative of giving up her job, or remaining under his roof! She longed to tell him haughtily that she had no intention of making any compromise, but somehow the idea of abandoning her work just when it had become so engrossing made it impossible for her to reject this ultimatum.

He drove in silence for a few minutes, then asked, 'Well, have you made up your mind? What do you choose to do?'

'I'll stay,' she told him flatly.

He nodded. 'Just what I thought you'd say! You're the kind of girl who sees a project through to the finish.'

There was an air of satisfaction about him that made her regret she had forgone the pleasure of giving an outright refusal.

Yet, as they drew up outside Drumdarrow and as she got out and once again entered its ancient doors, in spite of her protestations, she could not suppress a feeling of warm happiness; as though, she realised with a pang, she was returning to a well-loved home.

Suddenly, after the fatigues and excitements of the day, she felt utterly exhausted. And Graham, with his usual perspicacity, said quietly, 'I think you'd better go up now. I'll have something sent to your room. You look dead beat.'

At the unexpected gentleness in his voice, she felt tears flash to her eyes. Resolutely she blinked them back. It would be a mistake to let a man like Graham Lairdlaw realise how weak and irresolute she felt.

But she was helpless to prevent tears coursing down her cheeks.

He put an arm about her and drew her close against his shoulder.

'I know you've had a horrid day, Miranda. Don't you think it's time you and I tried to understand each other a little better?'

But she found it impossible to answer. She was only aware that she was close to his heart, and that his voice held a tenderness that filled her with intoxicating happiness.

It was just then that Shona chose to emerge from the small parlour. She stopped and stared disbelievingly and Miranda saw the faint pink fade from her cheeks.

'So you've brought her back! How could you!'

As she heard the words Miranda stared at Shona incredulously, for a strange transformation had come over Shona: the once childish, sweet treble was harsh with rage, and the large luminous eyes had darkened with venom. Miranda realised that, for the first time, she was seeing Shona without her mask of childlike naïveté. This was a woman filled with vicious rage and jealousy: there was something horrible and frightening about the metamorphosis.

She was grateful for Graham's arm about her, strong and comforting, and felt him draw her closer, as though sensing her reaction.

Then, as though realising that she had momentarily betrayed herself, Shona burst into a storm of tears and turning, fled back into the room.

After her departure, an uneasy silence lay between

158

them for a moment, then Graham gave a short laugh, and bending down, kissed Miranda lightly on the nose before releasing her.

'Don't look so tragic! The world really hasn't fallen on your head. I'm afraid Esther spoils Shona dreadfully and when she gets into a rage she's inclined to let herself rip. Luckily the storms don't last long. Now pop up to bed, and get a good night's sleep. You'll find that Shona will be her own sweet self again tomorrow.'

But just how much of this diagnosis of Shona did Graham himself believe? Miranda wondered, as she slowly climbed the stairs. Did he really imagine that Shona's display of vicious rage was no more than a momentary and regrettable lapse and that fundamentally she was still the gentle and charming girl that she appeared to be? But Miranda had now no such illusion. She was filled with a feeling of foreboding, for she realised that in Shona she had an implacable enemy.

On the following morning Miranda got up especially early and going to one of the cases in the gallery, took out a jewelled miniature of Madame de Maintenon: its diamond setting was badly in need of cleaning.

She had hardly settled down at her table in the workroom when, to her surprise, Shona came in.

She walked across the room with her rapid, graceful steps and in her high, almost childish treble said apologetically, 'I've just popped in to tell you how sorry I am about the horrid things I said last night. I can't imagine what came over me. Afterwards, when I thought about it, I really felt dreadful. I could hardly sleep a wink all night, wondering if you would ever forgive me. Actually, afterwards I was glad Graham insisted on fetching you back: things weren't the same without you. It's strange really, considering the size of the Castle, but even with one person missing it somehow feels empty. I expect it's because you've become like one of the family,' she added ingenuously. 'You do forgive me, don't you?' She stopped and looked at Miranda appealingly.

But without looking up Miranda calmly proceeded with her work. It was no longer possible for Shona to deceive her with those bewildering changes of attitude. Shona, when she had given vent to her rage and bitter jealousy on the previous evening, had revealed herself in her true colours: her charming, kittenish attitudes were no longer convincing. Shona was a dangerous tiger-cat, who at times showed her claws unsheathed.

When Miranda did not answer, Shona came up behind her and gazed over her shoulder.

'What are you working on?' she asked with an air of simulated interest.

'It's a miniature of Madame de Maintenon,' Miranda answered shortly.

'I must say she looks extremely prim and proper. I've a feeling she would hardly approve of me,' Shona added with a short laugh. 'Wasn't she the lady-friend of some French king or other?'

'Yes, she married Louis XIV privately.'

'Well, I can't imagine what he saw in her,' Shona remarked. 'She's not at all beautiful and looks deadly dull. I always thought Louis XIV had an eye for the ladies. It seems to me he slipped up when it came to Madame de Maintenon.'

'Well, you know the saying,' Miranda reminded her

dryly, 'Beauty is in the eye of the beholder.'

Shona shrugged. 'Oh, that's all tosh! A man will fall for a beautiful woman, no matter what she's like underneath.'

Miranda looked up at her with sudden attention. 'Is that what you really think?' she asked quietly.

Shona laughed shortly. 'But of course! And, let's face it, I'm well qualified to know. If a woman's beautiful and clever she can get a man to jump through hoops.'

So that was Shona's unspoken attitude towards Graham, Miranda was thinking, feeling slow anger.

She continued her work in silence, conscious that Shona was watching her narrowly.

'You're in love with Graham, aren't you?' Shona asked abruptly. And when Miranda did not reply, she went on, 'All right, don't answer if you don't want to, but I can tell, you know! A woman always can! The trouble is, I'm determined to marry him, which makes it awkward, doesn't it? I suggest we discuss this sensibly and come to an arrangement.'

She sank into a chair, crossed her graceful legs, and surveyed Miranda with narrowed eyes.

'What on earth do you mean?' Miranda demanded.

'I mean that two women living under the same roof, both of them in love with the same man, is an impossible situation which can't continue. I think you were foolish not to remain in one of the chalets: you could have been quite happy there. Andy's rather fun when he wants to be; I can assure you, you wouldn't have been bored. I know because at one time he and I were quite good friends.'

She swung her foot and surveyed Miranda through her long lashes; there could be no mistaking her meaning.

'Perhaps I didn't find Andy as entertaining as you did,' Miranda said shortly.

Shona raised her eyebrows. 'Perhaps he's not quite your type! But on the other hand, you can put out of your mind any idea of settling in here.'

'Don't worry, I shan't be here much longer,' Miranda told her coldly. 'As soon as the work is completed, I'm going back to London.'

'That's what you say, but will you, I wonder?'

'Why shouldn't I?' Miranda demanded impatiently.

'I mean, that no doubt, at present, you have every intention of doing that, but surely a part of you hopes that somehow or other things will work out for you and, just like a fairy-tale, Graham may come across you some day in the corridor and see beneath your Cinderella exterior the fairy princess of his dreams. I'll bet, at times,' she added, her voice thin with malice, 'you dream of yourself in an exquisite bridal gown, the wedding bells ringing, and Graham and yourself returning in triumph to Drumdarrow.'

Miranda coloured and turned her head away. What Shona had said held more than a hint of truth. In her secret heart did she not dream that in some mysterious way Graham would come to care for her?

'You see, you do hope!' Shona sneered. 'I can tell by your expression. A woman in love always hopes: she can't help it. But, Miranda, you should face up to things and realise that in Graham's life there is no place for you! I know this is going to sound horrid, but we may as well be frank! Aren't you—well, to put it mildly, a little Bohemian for Drumdarrow? You never would have fitted in, but now that Nigel has named Graham as his heir, it's completely out of the question.'

'Graham inherit Drumdarrow?' Miranda queried.

'Yes, Drumdarrow will belong to Graham. To manage a house like Drumdarrow needs experience and—let's face up to it—a certain background which I think you'll admit you definitely haven't got. Oh, I expect you thought you did wonders helping out with the children's party, but that's easy enough; entertaining Graham's friends and taking your place here as his wife would be quite a different matter. There are all sorts of little indescribable ways in which you could come a cropper, without even being aware of it. I know you won't be offended if I speak plainly; because you're such a terribly forthright sort of person one needn't mince one's words.'

'I hardly think little things like etiquette are important when a man and woman truly love one another,' Miranda said dryly.

'Oh, but that's where you're wrong! They are important! Terribly, terribly important,' Shona assured her. 'After all, you've seen only one side of Graham's character. But I've known him longer than you have. You've never seen him on really formal occasions. Let's suppose your wildest dreams were to come true and you were to marry Graham think how you'd feel when you found you didn't know the small, indefinable things that show whether a girl belongs or not. Graham, of course, would never bring the matter up, but I can assure you he'd notice, and gradually it would erode any chance of happiness you might have. You must take my word for this, Miranda, and put him out of your mind completely. I think you'll agree that I know him a lot better than you do.'

'Nonsense!' Miranda burst out. 'It just isn't in

Graham's character! He'd be completely contemptuous of those small, trivial snobberies!'

She felt suddenly that she had seen through Shona's gambit. The girl had been saying these things in an effort to convince her how hopeless her dreams might be; like a great general planning a battle and preceding it by taking steps to demoralize the enemy.

At Miranda's firm, almost contemptuous rejection of her little speech, Shona leapt to her feet, her eyes blazing. 'I see! So that's how it is! So it's going to be war to the hilt! Well, don't be surprised if things grow exceedingly uncomfortable for you! I've no intention of sitting back and allowing you to inveigle yourself into our lives. I can assure you that, much as you may dislike Andy Blair, you're going to regret that you ever left the chalet and returned to Drumdarrow.'

CHAPTER TEN

On the following morning Miranda resumed work on the miniature of Madame de Maintenon. She concentrated on it for a couple of hours and then strolled into the long gallery.

Kneeling on a red velvet cushion on one of the window seats, she gazed out. Although it was late autumn many of the trees still held their foliage and against the burnt orange of bracken and undergrowth formed a pattern of rich colour, from the deep velvety green of the conifers to the pale gold of weeping birch; the sky was cloudless, and the clear, pale blue of stretched silk. Not a breath of air broke the still enchantment of the scene. It was like an exquisite tapestry, Miranda thought, and remembered the line from *The Lady of the Lake*: how accurate Sir Walter Scott had been when he had described the Trossachs as:

'The scenery of a fairy dream.'

She felt a sudden overwhelming urge to abandon work and sample that cool, crystal air that had the heady delicious quality of a mountain stream.

She returned to the workroom and pulled off her overall. She was wearing a tweed dress and she knew a coat would be unnecessary; it would be almost warm outside, for here, even in late autumn, the air held a hint of golden sunshine.

She opened the drawer in her worktable where she kept Scott's poem and slipping it into her large patch pocket, left the Castle by a side door.

Following a narrow path she found her favourite spot, a little green grassy alcove in a grove of silver birch: a rustic bench was set in this secluded nook; nearby a tiny burn cascaded down between mossy stones, and tinkled out of sight through the thick bracken.

She had hardly begun to read when she heard the crunch of footsteps on the path. She looked through the tracery of branches and saw Graham stroll past; he was smoking a pipe and seemed oblivious of her presence.

She watched him eagerly, glad that for once she need not guard her expression, for she realised clearly now that she loved him.

Yet at no time had he seemed so unattainable. Only occasionally must he remember her presence there in the workroom. And when he did think of her——!

165

Well, to him no doubt she was only the girl he had employed to attend to the collection, a girl who, at times, had managed to prove herself an exasperating nuisance.

Then, to her consternation, Graham turned and looked directly at her. A faint, quizzical smile creased his eyes and for an instant she wondered if he had known for some time that she was there and that she had been watching his movements intently.

'Hello! And what are you doing there, gazing out like a wood-nymph—or should I say a field-mouse?'

He pushed the branches aside and joined her.

'I—I'm reading *The Lady of the Lake*,' she stammered. There was something faintly mocking in his manner that convinced her that he suspected she had quietly been watching him from her retreat. 'It's—it's such a lovely afternoon I thought I'd read for a bit, and——'

'And where have you got to?' he asked, ignoring her embarrassment, and taking the book from her fingers sat down beside her on the bench.

It only added to her confusion when, as he opened it, the book fell open at the flyleaf, where his own name and hers stood out in thick black letters.

He turned to the bookmarked page.

'I see you're at the part where Roderick Dhu and Malcolm Graeme are fighting over Ellen and her father parts them.'

> ' "What! is the Douglas fall'n so far,
> His daughter's hand is doom'd the spoil
> Of such dishonourable broil!" '

Miranda quoted softly.

'I see you know the lines, but you haven't read much of it so far, have you?'

'Oh, but I've finished it already,' she assured him quickly. 'I'm reading it again more slowly.'

'And have you made up your mind about Ellen's suitors? She's in the lucky position of having two men fighting for her favours. Which of them do you prefer? "Black Sir Roderick" whom she feared? She

> "shuddered at his brow of gloom,
>   His shadowy plaid, and sable plume;
>   His haughty mien and lordly air."

All in all he doesn't sound a very attractive character! Her other swain, Malcolm Graeme, must have seemed a welcome change! Surely you can have nothing against him?'

His eyes were dancing with amusement as he quoted the description of Ellen's young lover.

> ' "His flaxen hair of sunny hue,
>   Curl'd closely round his bonnet blue.
>   His form accorded with a mind
>   Lively and ardent, frank and kind".'

And then Miranda took up the quotation.

> ' "A blither heart, till Ellen came,
>   Did never love nor sorrow tame." '

'There, you see! The ideal man, in fact!' Graham said solemnly. 'Scott makes it quite plain, when he says,

"... of his clan, in hall and bower,
    Young Malcolm Graeme was held the
flower." '

He closed the book and handed it back to her. 'One doesn't-like to boast, but sometimes I fancy I possess something of the characteristics of my namesake. You see, Graeme is the early spelling of Graham.'

'But you're not a bit like him!' Miranda burst out impulsively. 'If anything, you resemble Roderick Dhu.'

He flung back his head in a sudden shout of laughter. 'So you shudder at my brow of gloom! I really didn't think I had that effect on you. However, I agree with you as far as Roderick Dhu is concerned; I'm not very keen on brows of gloom myself. On the other hand, you can't afford to criticise Roderick, you know! You're not, by any chance, under the impression that you're remotely like sweet Ellen? Although in one respect you do have something in common.'

'And what is that?' she asked, trying to keep the eagerness out of her voice.

He turned his head, and looking at her directly, said softly, 'In "thine eye's dark witchcraft".'

She laughed awkwardly. Then realised that the thrill of happiness she had experienced at his words must have been reflected in her expression.

She turned away and began to tug at some ferny fronds that grew nearby. 'Oh, I know I'm not like Ellen,' she began airily, 'but at the same time——'

'But at the same time, you see yourself as gentle, kind, docile—everything, in fact, that you're not! The trouble with you, Miranda, is that you're wilful, unco-operative, and have a touch of the termagant.'

168

'What?' she exploded, swinging around on the seat and staring at him indignantly.

'All right! All right! Don't go up in a spiral! To be quite truthful, I find sweet-natured, polite girls rather a bore.'

'Thanks!' she snapped. 'but I'm not particularly interested.'

'And what's more, you don't give a hoot what I think! Is that what you're going to tell me? Really I have to be very careful what I say to you, haven't I?'

'That's not true!' she protested. 'I'm not the least bit like——' She stopped. Not the least bit like Shona, she had been on the point of saying.

Shona, who was so touchy that everyone went in dread of setting off one of her hysterical outbursts, or a flood of tears! Not, of course, that this was indeed Shona's true character. She had made it only too plain on the previous day that this was only a façade and that she was a girl who believed in getting her own way by hook or by crook, and simply used her tears and temperamental outbursts to achieve her own ends.

Graham continued, as if he hadn't noticed her abrupt halt. 'Why, if you're such an equitable, placid sort of person did you hare off to the chalet? And I've no guarantee that at some future date you won't light out even further afield.'

'There's not much use in my setting myself up in chalets—or anywhere else for that matter, if you're going to come and fetch me back again. Although "fetch" is rather too mild a word to express your methods,' she retorted tartly.

'Yes, and I'll always fetch you back, no matter how far you go, Miranda!' His voice was low, but held a fierce resolve.

Miranda held her breath. Had she only imagined the wealth of tenderness that lay behind those brusquely spoken words? Did he really mean he would always seek her out no matter how far she strayed from Drumdarrow?

'Graham!' Shona's clear, high voice trilled and there was the sound of her quick, light steps on the gravelled path.

Miranda felt a wave of sickening disappointment engulf her as Shona pushed aside the light branches and joined them.

She looked from one to another with an air of bright inquiry. 'Am I interrupting something? I'd hate to butt in if it's private.'

'You're not interrupting anything,' Graham told her shortly.

And Miranda wondered if she had only imagined that his voice held boredom. Was it possible that Shona's everlasting little-girl naïveté had at last begun to pall on him?

'Well, what is it this time? I can see from the expression on your face that there's something you want me to do for you. Am I right?'

Shona pouted coyly. 'You can be horrid when you want to, Graham. You know you promised to take a look at the car and let me know if it ought to be sent in for overhaul.'

He gazed at her for a moment in silence, and there could be no mistaking the look of quizzical impatience on his face. 'Now don't be a baby, Shona! All you have to do is to take a look at the mileage. That will tell you immediately. There's no necessity for me to take a hand in it.'

'But you know how I hate doing that sort of thing

by myself! Anyway,' she added sweetly, 'aren't you flattered that I came in search of you?'

'Oh, very well!' he said resignedly. 'I suppose being indispensable is a compliment of sorts.'

'But of course it is!' Her mouth curved into a smile showing her small perfect teeth and she pushed back a tendril of silver-blonde hair.

'I shan't ask you to accompany us to look at the speedometer,' he told Miranda with a wry smile. 'You would hardly find it fascinating. But if you read on you'll find that Ellen and her father go into hiding in the hollow of the mountain, a haunted place where

> "fays resort,
>   And satyrs hold their silvan court,
>   By moonlight tread their mystic maze." '

Shona giggled. 'You haven't been reading poetry together, have you? How utterly quaint! Somehow I've never considered you a poetic type, Graham. But then perhaps Miranda brings the poet out in you!'

'Perhaps!' he agreed shortly. 'And now let's get this business of yours over and done with!'

And, somewhat ungraciously, he set off with Shona in the direction of the house.

When they had gone Miranda didn't continue reading. She had a bitter sense of anticlimax. If only Shona had not put in her appearance at that particular moment, for she had the feeling that she and Graham had been on the point of reaching a new and exciting relationship. Yet common sense forced her to acknowledge that as soon as Shona had put in her appearance Graham, although he had put up what was probably a show of reluctance, had gone away with her willingly

171

enough. As they went Shona had been clinging to his arm and laughing up into his face.

She must not indulge in wishful thinking, Miranda told herself. The fact that he liked to speak to her from time to time meant no more than that they had some interests in common. Yet, in the end, it was beautiful, empty-headed Shona whose smallest word could lead him where she wished.

As to Shona's discovery of them in the grove—that was no mystery! Miranda knew that this part of the grounds was overlooked by some of the upper rooms. No doubt Shona had seen Graham leave the house and had watched curiously to see in what direction his steps had taken him. She would then set about concocting an excuse for seeking him out and after a suitable interval had casually strolled out to join him.

When, later on, Miranda returned to the house she was in no mood for an encounter with Esther Gregg. But it was impossible to escape the woman, because as Miranda crossed the hall she was intercepted. Blocking the stairs with her substantial form, Esther faced Miranda belligerently.

'Don't you think you'd be better employed applying yourself to your work than in gallivanting about in the garden?' she demanded.

Miranda could feel her temper rising at this gratuitous attack. 'My movements are no concern of yours, Mrs Gregg. I was employed by Mr Lairdlaw. You have nothing whatsoever to do with my affairs.'

'Oh yes, I have, my girl!' Esther told her sharply. 'When it comes to your flinging yourself at Graham's head, and making my niece unhappy, it is very much my business. Your walk in the garden was only an excuse for a meeting with him.'

'Just as I thought,' Miranda said contemptuously, 'Shona has been spying, hasn't she?'

'Spying?' Esther laughed hoarsely. 'So that's what you call my niece's efforts to see that Graham is not embarrassed by your open efforts to attract his attention! Do you realise you're throwing yourself at the head of the man Shona is practically engaged to? No doubt, to a girl in your position, there's always the hope of catching the eye of her employer, but I can assure you that in real life these things don't happen— particularly in Graham Lairdlaw's case! Like every other man, he may be momentarily attracted by a pretty face, but he comes of a proud race and the idea of making a girl in your position mistress of Drumdarrow simply wouldn't enter his head, so don't waste your time pursuing him, there's no future in it as far as you're concerned, my girl!'

But Miranda's temper was aroused; she felt she had taken as much of Esther Gregg as she could endure.

'If what you say is true,' she replied contemptuously, 'then it appears to me that this conversation is pretty pointless. Besides, as you pointed out, I've work to do and you're wasting my time.'

She was conscious of the look of outrage on Esther's face as she slipped past her and ran upstairs. But once in her room she felt her momentary belligerence drain away.

She paced up and down her room, feeling that had Esther been aware of her plans she would have felt there was every justification for her accusation that she was neglecting her work, for with an almost fierce resolve she was determined to take the rest of the day off. Suddenly that big workroom, silent and lonely and cut off from the life of the rest of the house, seemed like an intolerable prison. She would go into Stirling; window-shop, make a few purchases perhaps; anything, to get away from Drumdarrow and its insoluble problems.

Giving herself no time to change her mind, she ran downstairs and phoned for a taxi, feeling a little guilty at such extravagance. But at least she could return by bus in the afternoon, she told herself.

She ran upstairs again, brushed her hair until it shone and slipped a coat over her tweed dress.

She waited in one of the embrasures in the long gallery until she saw the taxi approach along the drive, then snatching up her gloves and purse, she went straight downstairs—and right into Graham's arms.

'Well, we are in a hurry, aren't we? And where exactly are you off to?' he inquired.

He sounded casual and good-humoured, but his eyes demanded an answer.

'I—I've some shopping I simply must do,' she stammered. 'I thought I'd go into Stirling. You don't mind, do you? I suppose I should have asked, but——'

'You've earned an afternoon off,' he returned pleasantly. 'That workroom of yours can be pretty gloomy and lonely at this time of year. I suppose it gets you down at times!'

So he hadn't been deceived by her garbled excuse of a shopping expedition! But then she knew by this time that it was extremely hard to pull the wool over Graham Lairdlaw's eyes.

'Who knows, if you stay up there much longer, you may turn into a pretty and charming fossil.'

As he spoke he pulled out his wallet and handed her some notes. 'If you're going shopping, you'll probably need some cash.'

Miranda drew back. 'But I've plenty,' she protested.

He smiled. 'I'd forgotten you're a proud and haughty lady. Well, won't you accept it, just this once, and buy something pretty, something you'd really like? Be frivolous, for once, Miranda! There must be something your heart desires and that you sternly deny yourself.'

He was laughing at her, she knew. So he considered her prim! But somehow she didn't resent it. On the contrary, it was an indication that he understood her more deeply than she had realised.

She glanced back at him mischievously. 'Are those your orders, sir?' she asked demurely.

'They certainly are! And remember, when you come back, I want to see proof that you have obeyed my instructions.'

In Stirling, Miranda window-shopped: for a while she admired the beautiful silver-work done in the Hebrides incorporating the semi-precious jewels to be found in the mountains of Scotland. The shops that specialised in Scottish tweeds and knitwear she found completely engrossing: the hand-woven tartans, deliberately faded into exquisitely subtle hues to represent the colours of the kilts as they had been discovered after the battle of Culloden. The shops that catered for the tourists offered a fascinating variety of objects—skean dhus with silver filigree sheaths; sporrans of leather and deerskin; Edinburgh rock in tartan boxes, and a multitude of garishly coloured souvenirs.

After a while, tiring of this, she went to have tea and lingered over it as long as possible.

Afterwards, as she resumed her stroll through the

town she knew that this outing was not proving a success. The afternoon, in contrast to the morning, was overcast and there was a threat of rain in the low-hanging, grey clouds. She realised that she was not enjoying herself; without a companion, her expedition seemed pointless, and the crowded streets somehow seemed to accentuate her isolation.

To pass the time she bought a few items; handkerchiefs and stockings, and a climber's pom-pomed woollen cap to wear in the colder weather that would lie ahead. For Mrs Gilmore she bought a large box of chocolates with yellow and crimson roses on the lid which was surmounted by a yellow satin bow. Chocolates were one of the housekeeper's weaknesses, she knew, and for the first time since she had set out on her expedition, she felt a little glow of satisfaction as she tucked the parcelled box under her arm.

She would have time before the bus set off to take Graham's advice and treat herself to something pretty and impractical: she returned to one of the craft shops that specialised in Scottish silver work where earlier her eye had been caught by a pair of beautifully worked silver and amethyst ear-rings. Through the window it had been impossible to decipher their price, as the ticket that hung from them was discreetly minute.

When she went into the shop, she was rather appalled to discover how expensive they were, but when she had handled them and had seen how beautifully they were worked she found it impossible to resist the temptation of owning them.

After all, she told herself as she took her seat in the bus, it was in an indirect sort of way, a present from Graham. But how different from the presents he gave to Shona! How carefully he selected the bright, sparkling gems that she loved so much! And if Graham demanded to see her purchase, as he had threatened to do, would her choice, in comparison to Shona's taste, appear to him drab and unbecoming.

A sullen misty rain began to fall out of the grey, leaden sky as the bus pulled out of Stirling, and very shortly a pall of darkness fell over the countryside. Miranda, lost in her own thoughts, was dimly aware that the beat of the engine was uneven, and it was only when an ominous loud knocking sound began to reverberate through the bus that she sat up and began to take notice. The bus drew to a halt and an ominous silence ensued. They were on a lonely stretch of road running through bleak moors and it seemed there was every possibility of their being there for some time.

When the driver had hailed an approaching car and had given the message, he returned to inform them cheerfully that no doubt a relief bus would be along very shortly. The passengers, however, did not seem to share his optimism as they settled down to wait in morose silence, shivering in the cold bleakness of the damp autumn evening. When eventually the relief bus came in sight and they had transferred to it with their various packages and parcels it was quite dark.

As they drove into the little hamlet of Drumdarrow Miranda sat on the edge of her seat straining her eyes for the piers of the Castle gates picked up in the lights of the bus.

When she had alighted, clutching her parcels, and the bright lights of the bus had swept off and disappeared around a bend, she found that she was standing in stygian darkness.

Luckily the iron-wrought gates stood open, so she

didn't have to struggle with them: she entered the drive and began to pick her way along, hoping she would not blunder into the bushes on either side. Here she was sheltered from the bitterly cold breeze that was sweeping along the road and in silence and darkness she edged along.

But she had gone only a few steps when to her horror a hand gripped her arm and a voice spoke in her ear; she gave a scream of terror before she realised that it was Graham.

'Oh, it's you!' She was almost sobbing with relief, she was so delighted to know he was near.

But his mood did not match hers. 'Where have you been all this time?' he demanded. 'Do you realise how worried we've all been about you?'

'I was in Stirling,' she began. 'I told you——'

'Yes, you told me you were going into Stirling—to shop,' he interrupted. 'But it's fairly clear you weren't particularly interested in shopping. The whole town must have been shut up ages ago. What were you really doing?'

'But I—I *was* shopping,' she reiterated, unnerved by his barely controlled rage.

'You haven't been spending the time with Andy?' he demanded.

So that was how he had interpreted her obvious excuse to get away from the Castle! He thought that she had made a mere pretence of going to Stirling and had actually arranged to meet Andy!

'I suppose you didn't notice the time passing in his fascinating company,' Graham grated. 'Your conversation was so engrossing, no doubt!'

'But you know how I loathe Andy,' she protested.

'Do you, I wonder? You seemed to be on exceedingly good terms with him down at the chalet on the evening I so rudely interrupted.'

He was in no mood to listen to any explanations, she realised, and retreated into silence as they walked the length of the drive. Much to her annoyance, he kept his firm grip on her arm: as though, she thought resentfully, he was escorting a prisoner to one of the Drumdarrow dungeons.

As they reached the house she broke from his grasp and raced upstairs. She tossed her purchases on to a chair and flung herself down on her bed.

What a terrible fiasco this afternoon's outing had been! Her attempt to get away from the Castle and banish her mood of dull despondency for a short time had ended disastrously. What on earth was the matter with Graham; why had he taken that attitude? she wondered dully. Perhaps he had quarrelled with Shona, and had been venting his anger on her! The thought made her even more wretched. Shona had been right, she felt: two women living in the same house and both in love with the same man was a recipe for unhappiness. It was obvious one of them would have to go, and it was equally obvious that it was she who must take the first step. As soon as the work was finished, she told herself she would go, knowing that this was a comforting respite.

As her thoughts turned to the work ahead, she remembered with a start that she had not returned the miniature of Madame de Maintenon to the case, but had left it on the work-table.

She hurried to the work-room and switched on the lights; then she crossed to her table, set in the oriel window. She had left the miniature on the flat circle of leather filled with sand that she used when working metal, but there was no sign of it and frantically she began to search the room, pulling out drawers, and opening cupboards. She dropped to her knees and searched the shadowed floor under the table, but even as she did so she had the leaden feeling that her search was hopeless.

She got to her feet and tried to control her rising panic. The jewelled miniature was valuable. Had there been a burglary while she was out? She sped into the gallery where a quick examination assured her that everything was in its place: nothing but the miniature was missing. But why? she wondered. Surely if there had been a robbery the intruder would have helped himself to some of the other valuable items!

Then suddenly she knew what had become of the precious trinket.

She remembered Shona standing behind her as she explained that the enamelled face was that of Madame de Maintenon; remembered Shona, knowing that her pose of sweet girlish innocence had been seen through, spitting out vindictively that from now on it would be war to the hilt between them.

And with dreadful clarity Miranda could see what Shona hoped to achieve by removing the miniature.

Almost certainly Graham would hold her responsible for its loss. Would he remember too how, when he had first employed her, he had known almost nothing of her background?

Well, she would not tamely allow herself to be driven from Drumdarrow, branded as a thief.

She did not allow herself to pause to consider the situation more coolly, because if she did, she suspected, her resolve would melt away. Seething with indignation, she ran downstairs and burst into the

180

small parlour.

A scene of cosy domesticity met her. Shona was sitting at a table near a floor-lamp, her hands poised over a jigsaw puzzle; Graham was seated in a leather armchair by the fire engrossed in a book.

At her precipitous entry, he looked up at her in mild inquiry. 'If I didn't know that Drumdarrow was unhaunted, I'd say you'd seen nothing less than a headless horseman.'

So he had got over his black mood, Miranda was thinking. Perhaps he had made up whatever quarrel with Shona had made him so bitterly angry when she had returned from Stirling!

But still possessed by a seething rage, she swung on Shona. 'Well, where is it?' she demanded.

Deliberately the girl fitted in a piece of the jigsaw, then inquired with a faintly aggrieved air, 'Really, Miranda, what on earth are you talking about? Do please come in and shut the door. There's a beastly draught.'

Miranda, meeting the wide limpid stare of those gentian-blue eyes, felt her anger evaporate and with it all hope of confronting Shona and wringing the truth from her. But it was too late to draw back. 'I'm talking about the miniature of Madame de Maintenon—what have you done with it?'

Shona gave one of her light, guileless trills of laughter and turned appealingly to Graham. 'Do you understand what this is all about? It sounds like double-Dutch to me.'

Graham laid his book aside and regarded Miranda with grave attention. 'I must say I agree—you're not making yourself very plain, Miranda,' he said, a slight line between his brows. 'And what is all the excitement about? Surely you can say whatever you have to say without all the melodrama.'

Miranda bit her lip. By her foolish and precipitate behaviour she had placed herself in a ridiculous and humiliating position.

As slowly and as calmly as she could she said, 'When I returned this evening I discovered that the miniature of Madame de Maintenon was missing.'

Graham got to his feet abruptly. 'Missing? Do you mean the gallery has been broken into?'

'No—no, it—it wasn't in the gallery,' Miranda admitted hesitantly, feeling as though the ground were opening under her feet.

'Not in the gallery? Then where on earth was it?' he asked impatiently.

'I—I left it on the table in the work-room,' Miranda admitted.

There was silence in the small room: the wood fire hissed and crackled. Then, in a small voice, Shona said, 'And you thought I took it!'

And Miranda, seeing the familiar look of hurt bewilderment creep into Shona's face, was thinking what an excellent actress the girl was. No doubt in a moment tears would course from those wide eyes in a pathetic appeal, she thought with detached contempt.

Graham's voice broke in, sharp and derisive. 'If the miniature is missing, then you are responsible. You must have mislaid it; put it down somewhere and forgotten about it. Why haven't you the guts to admit you're in the wrong, instead of accusing Shona?'

Miranda stared at him, feeling the blood ebb from her face.

Then unexpectedly, he said, 'Sit down, I can see you've had a great shock.' His voice had lost its harshness. 'I suggest we talk this over as calmly as possible. You've very probably put it down somewhere. It must be among the odds and ends you keep in the table drawers. After all, it's not a large item, it would be quite easy to mislay it. I suggest you try to remember your movements, and then make a thorough search.'

'But I have,' Miranda told him through dry lips. 'I've looked everywhere; I've searched thoroughly and there's no sign of it.'

Again silence fell on the room.

'I see,' he said with an air of dry finality. 'In other words you're telling me that the miniature is gone for good.'

'Which doesn't surprise me in the least,' Shona put in. 'This afternoon you tear off to Stirling and now, on your return, you conveniently discover that the miniature is missing. The whole thing strikes me as being remarkably fishy.'

'Oh, Shona, do be quiet!' Graham said shortly.

But she was not to be silenced.

'She's as good as accused me of stealing the wretched thing,' Shona protested. 'Surely I've a right to defend myself? And what do you know about her anyway? You chose to believe whatever she told you. After all, she could be a——'

'That's enough!' Graham interposed brusquely.

But Miranda was in no doubt about what the unspoken word had been. Shona had been on the point of calling her a thief. She didn't want to hear any more. Sick at heart, she turned and crept from the room. As she shut the door quietly behind her she could hear Shona's voice, shrill and accusing; it seemed to follow her as she slowly climbed the stairs.

She returned to the work-room, but knowing it was

183

hopeless to pursue the search, paced up and down agitatedly. Nothing seemed to lie before her but ignominious ejection from Drumdarrow. Although, at the moment, Graham seemed to have an open mind concerning the loss of the miniature he was bound, sooner or later, to agree with Shona that he had taken her on knowing very little about her or her background. Soon he might come to think that she had staged the little scene in an effort to divert suspicion from herself.

Suddenly she halted her restless pacing and clenched her hands in determination as she made up her mind that she would not leave without making one last attempt to clear her name.

In all probability the trinket would be in Shona's room. Now would be an excellent time to search for it, while Shona was downstairs with Graham, eagerly pointing out to him that there could be only one explanation for its disappearance.

Perhaps if she had been in a calmer frame of mind she might have hesitated before taking such a step, but the searing thought that Graham might, in time, come to accept Shona's views of her character spurred her on.

She hurried along the corridor to Shona's room and, flinging open the door, switched on the lights. Then her heart sank as she surveyed the large bedroom, for it was littered with a variety of small objects.

Shona's dressing-table held a clutter of photographs, tiny glass animals, bottles of make-up. One framed photograph on the table beside her bed showed her with Graham; they were skating together against a wintry background of snow-laden fir trees; in another photograph they were in bathing-dress, reclining on white sands, Shona's curls dazzlingly fair against tanned skin.

Feverishly Miranda pulled open drawers and ransacked the bureau, turning over piles of filmy negligées and the expensive silk stockings that were one of Shona's extravagances. She jumped on to a chair and ran her hands over the top of the wardrobe; then tackled the interior of the wardrobe itself, feeling in the pockets of winter sportswear and costumes and briefly marvelling at the extent of the girl's wardrobe.

But her search was hopeless, she realised. It would take much too long to examine all Shona's possessions. An article as small as the miniature could be hidden in almost any place in this large cluttered room. With a feeling of blank despair, she pushed in a drawer that did not fully close, and realising what a horrible scene would certainly ensue should Shona catch her rifling her possessions, she abandoned her effort to shut it. She snapped off the lights and stepped out into the corridor.

It was just at this moment that Shona came in view, and saw her hesitating in the doorway.

'What were you doing in my room?' she demanded belligerently.

Miranda, stricken into silence by the realisation of how contemptible her actions must seem, did not reply, and Shona stared at her with narrowed eyes. 'Why, I believe you've been searching my room.'

She pushed past Miranda and stood looking about her room.

And Miranda, knowing that the signs of her intrusion must be only too apparent, walked quickly along the corridor and began to descend the stairs. Why had she allowed anger and wounded pride to lead her into such a hideous situation? she asked herself, her cheeks burning with mortification. She longed to be outdoors in the cool, clean, fresh air.

But she had reckoned without Shona.

She heard the sound of the girl's heels on the stairs and Shona caught her arm in a surprisingly firm grip. 'So you *were* searching my room!' she shrilled. 'Well, don't think you'll get away with it! Graham shall hear how you sneaked into my room and turned it upside-down.'

'And what exactly is Graham going to hear?'

His appearance in the doorway of the small parlour momentarily silenced Shona, then she said angrily, 'I just want you to know that, not satisfied with stealing the miniature, Miranda has ransacked my bedroom.'

'I think both of you had better come in here and let's talk this business over as quietly and rationally as possible,' Graham instructed.

When they had entered, he shut the door firmly and turned to Miranda. 'And now, what's all this nonsense about your searching Shona's room?'

'It's not nonsense,' Shona began.

'Be quiet,' he snapped so brusquely that her eyes flashed angrily, but she subsided into a sulky silence.

'Now, what have you to say?' he demanded of Miranda.

'Yes, it's true,' she replied.

'But why?'

She knew that he was genuinely puzzled. Her action seemed inexplicable to him.

She drew a deep breath. 'I did it because I believe Shona has the miniature,' she told him.

'You must be aware that what you're saying is untrue,' he said with biting contempt.

At this juncture Shona burst into a peal of hysterical laughter. 'To think of me stealing such a tatty old object! What would I do with it anyway? Why, I've more jewellery than I can wear! Aunt Esther is always giving me presents—and you too, Graham.'

'I'm not saying you stole the miniature,' Miranda told her. 'You deliberately took it, knowing I'd be suspected of stealing it. After all,' she added dryly, 'as you pointed out, Graham knows very little about me.'

To her relief her voice sounded steady and assured and she was aware of Graham watching her searchingly.

It was then that Shona chose to revert to the role that she felt so well became her. She jumped to her feet, ran across the room and clung to Graham, her face raised appealingly to his.

'Oh, Graham, you mustn't keep her on, not after all the dreadful things she's said!' she cried in a quivering voice, her eyes flooding with tears.

She reached in her pocket and pulled out a lace-edged handkerchief; something small and glittering was caught in its border, and next instant the little enamel and diamond miniature had fallen to the carpet at her feet.

For a long minute there was absolute silence in the room and Miranda noticed that Shona's face had grown pallid as she stared down at the trinket as though hypnotised.

Then, with deliberation, Graham stooped and retrieved it. For a moment he held it thoughtfully in the palm of his hand, then turned to Shona with an expression on his face that unmistakably announced the death-knell of her plans.

Shona stared at him, wide-eyed, then opened her

mouth as though to plead with him. Instead, as though realising the hopelessness of her position, she gave a little inarticulate cry, and turning, fled from the room.

When she had gone, Miranda and Graham faced each other across the room. And suddenly the tensions and emotions of the previous few hours surged up, and Miranda found herself sobbing helplessly.

Afterwards, she was never to know how it happened, but his arms were about her and her head was pressed against his heart, and she realised she was ecstatically happy.

'Sorry,' she sniffed apologetically, 'I really don't make a habit of dissolving into tears.'

'Well, goodness knows, you've ample excuse to cry,' he said. 'If I remember rightly, I was extremely nasty about Andy Blair.'

'Yes, you were,' she agreed.

He chuckled. 'That's my familiar old Miranda, full of the fighting spirit! But, as regards Andy, I'm afraid it was plain jealousy. You see, I thought you'd fallen for him. Although, now that I come to think of it, it was foolish of me,' he added solemnly, 'because I'm obviously so much more attractive.'

Miranda laughed through her tears. 'I do believe you really think that!'

'Not altogether,' he assured her. 'I think I'll always be a little jealous where you're concerned, my darling.'

He felt in his pocket for the miniature and placing it in her hand folded her fingers firmly over it. 'I want you to have this. After all, it brought us together. I only hope our marriage will be as happy as dear old Madame de Maintenon's was.'

But Miranda's eyes were fixed on the piece of tartan

ribbon that he had pulled out with the miniature. 'My ribbon! So you kept it!' she whispered.

He nodded and replaced it carefully in his pocket. 'It will remain there,' he told her. 'close to my heart— as you are now.'

Send for your copy today!

The Harlequin Romance Catalog FREE!

Here's your chance to catch up on all the wonderful Harlequin Romance novels you may have missed because the books are no longer available at your favorite booksellers.

Complete the coupon and mail it to us. By return mail, we'll send you a copy of the latest Harlequin catalog. Then you'll be able to order the books you want directly from us.

Clip and mail coupon today.

40 magnificent Omnibus volumes to choose from:

Essie Summers #1
Bride in Flight (#933)
Postscript to Yesterday (#1119)
Meet on My Ground (#1326)

Jean S. MacLeod
The Wolf of Heimra (#990)
Summer Island (#1314)
Slave of the Wind (#1339)

Eleanor Farnes
The Red Cliffs (#1335)
The Flight of the Swan (#1280)
Sister of the Housemaster (#975)

Susan Barrie #1
Marry a Stranger (#1034)
Rose in the Bud (#1168)
The Marriage Wheel (#1311)

Violet Winspear #1
Beloved Tyrant (#1032)
Court of the Veils (#1267)
Palace of the Peacocks (#1318)

Isobel Chace
The Saffron Sky (#1250)
A Handful of Silver (#1306)
The Damask Rose (#1334)

Joyce Dingwell #1
Will You Surrender (#1179)
A Taste for Love (#1229)
The Feel of Silk (#1342)

Sara Seale
Queen of Hearts (#1324)
Penny Plain (#1197)
Green Girl (#1045)

Jane Arbor
A Girl Named Smith (#1000)
Kingfisher Tide (#950)
The Cypress Garden (#1336)

Anne Weale
The Sea Waif (#1123)
The Feast of Sara (#1007)
Doctor in Malaya (#914)

Essie Summers #2
His Serene Miss Smith (#1093)
The Master to Tawhai (#910)
A Place Called Paradise (#1156)

Catherine Airlie
Doctor Overboard (#979)
Nobody's Child (#1258)
A Wind Sighing (#1328)

Violet Winspear #2
Bride's Dilemma (#1008)
Tender Is the Tyrant (#1208)
The Dangerous Delight (#1344)

Kathryn Blair
Doctor Westland (#954)
Battle of Love (#1038)
Flowering Wilderness (#1148)

Rosalind Brett
The Girl at White Drift (#1101)
Winds of Enchantment (#1176)
Brittle Bondage (#1319)

Rose Burghley
Man of Destiny (#960)
The Sweet Surrender (#1023)
The Bay of Moonlight (#1245)

Iris Danbury
Rendezvous in Lisbon (#1178)
Doctor at Villa Ronda (#1257)
Hotel Belvedere (#1331)

Amanda Doyle
A Change for Clancy (#1085)
Play the Tune Softly (#1116)
A Mist in Glen Torran (#1308)

Great value in Reading!
Use the handy order form